DEATH IN SPRINGTIME

Also by the author

DEATH OF AN ENGLISHMAN
DEATH OF A DUTCHMAN
DEATH IN AUTUMN
THE MARSHAL AND THE MURDERER
THE MARSHAL AND THE MADWOMAN
THE MARSHAL'S OWN CASE
THE MARSHAL MAKES HIS REPORT
THE MARSHAL AT THE VILLA TORRINI
THE MONSTER OF FLORENCE
PROPERTY OF BLOOD
SOME BITTER TASTE
THE INNOCENT

with Paolo Vagheggi
THE PROSECUTOR

Death in Springtime

Magdalen Nabb

Copyright © 1983 by Magdelen Nabb
and 1999 by Diogenes Verlag AG Zurich

Pubished in the United States in 2005 by
Soho Press, Inc.
853 Broadway
New York, NY 10003

All rights reserved.

Library of Congress Cataloging in Publication Data

Nabb, Magdalen, 1947-
Death in springtime / Magdalen Nabb
p. cm.
ISBN-13: 978-1-56947-415-0
ISBN-10: 1-56947-415-X

1. Guarnaccia, Marshal (Ficticious character)–Fiction. 2. Young women–Crimes against–Fiction. 3. Police–Italy–Florence–Fiction. 4. Americans–Italy–Fiction. 5. Florence (Italy)–Fiction. 6. Kidnapping–Fiction. I. Title.

PR6064.A18D37 2005
823'.914–dc22 2005049045

10 9 8 7 6 5 4 3 2

A LETTER FROM GEORGES SIMENON

Dear friend and fellow author,

What a pleasure it is to wander with you through the streets of Florence, with their carabinieri, working people, trattorie, even their noisy tourists. It is all so alive: its sounds audible, its smells as perceptible as the light morning mist above the Arno's swift current; and then up into the foothills, where the Sardinian shepherds, their traditions and the almost unchanged rhythm of their lifestyle, are just as skilfully portrayed. What wouldn't one give to taste one of their ricotta cheeses!

You have managed to absorb it all and to depict it vividly, whether it is the various ranks of the carabinieri, and of course the ineffable Substitute Prosecutor, or the trattorie in the early morning hours. There is never a false note. You even capture that shimmer in the air which is so peculiar to this city and to the still untamed countryside close at hand.

This is a novel to be savoured, even more than its two predecessors. It is the first time I have seen the theme of kidnapping treated so simply and so plausibly. Although the cast of characters is large, they are so well etched in a few words that their comings and goings are easily followed.

Bravissimo! You have more than fulfilled your promise.

Georges Simenon

Lausanne, April 1983

CHAPTER 1

'It can't be. Today's the first of March . . .'

'But it is, look!'

'Must be some sort of seed blowing on the wind.'

'What wind? I tell you it's snow!'

The entire population of Florence had woken up blinking in amazement and consternation. Shutters had banged open and people had exclaimed to one another across courtyards and narrrow streets.

'It's snowing!'

Only once in the last fifteen years or so had it snowed in the city, and that had been in the middle of winter when an icy blast from the Russian Steppes had swept across the whole Italian peninsula, covering even the motorways with a paralysing blanket of white. But today was the first of March. And to make it even more incredible the weather during the past two weeks had been exceptionally warm, and the first tourists, always the ones from Germany, had been going about in light-coloured clothing, the women baring plump white arms to the feverish February sun. The Florentines themselves never shed their green loden overcoats until the end of April, but even so, a few people had been sufficiently deceived to put the first potted geraniums out on their windowsills, and in the mild evenings brown slatted shutters had been left half-open to reveal bands of yellow light and silhouetted figures looking out to watch the goings on in the piazza, giving the impression of a summer night.

Then it had only been the vine- and wheat-growers in the surrounding hills who had complained about the weather. After all, at that time of year it ought to have been raining. Now, to cap everything, it was snowing, and people couldn't have been more surprised if carnival confetti had been falling out of the sky.

The eight o'clock rush hour had started under the stare of a pale cold light. Toddlers pressed their noses against windows high up in lighted apartments making patches of steam which they rubbed away or drew in with one finger.

The sky was so blank that the snow seemed to be falling down from nowhere, appearing between the great stone buildings, big wet flakes that floated into the road and vanished, leaving only a mottled damp strip between the dry pavements and gutters which were sheltered by the overhanging eaves.

People queuing for the bus in the tiny Piazza San Felice turned up their collars and looked anxiously at the sky, wondering if perhaps they should have worn a scarf or gloves. But it wasn't even cold! There was no explanation for it at all. Opposite them, Marshal Guarnaccia of The Carabinieri was standing on the corner as he often did after having a coffee at the bar. He stood on the edge of a group of gossiping mothers who had just given their children over to the care of a nun who ushered them into the infant school next to the church, and he alone, although he turned up the collar of his black greatcoat with an automatic gesture, was not staring at the snow but at the trattoria across the street. Over there the lights were on in clusters of hanging globes, and the owner's son, wrapped in a dirty white apron, was sweeping up in a desultory fashion, scattering sawdust just behind the glass door, staring out vacantly at the weather all the while. The boy, thin and pimply with a shock of black hair, was only sixteen, but already Marshal Guarnaccia had caught sight of him injecting himself on the steps of Santo Spirito church, sitting on the edge of the usual huddled group and glancing furtively about him in a way that only very new users do.

The number 15 bus came along and stopped, blocking

the Marshal's view. The bus, too, was lit up, and every face along its length was gazing out as if hypnotized by the big flakes floating slowly down past the windows. The Marshal, preoccupied with the problem of what, if anything, to say to the boy's father, and with a case that was coming up in Appeal Court in a few days, continued to ignore the snow, even though, as a Sicilian, he might well have been more amazed by it than the Florentines. Nevertheless, he was destined to remember it only too well and to be driven to exasperation by witness after witness repeating the same infuriating phrase with the same apologetic smile:

'I didn't notice anything, to be honest. I don't know if you remember but it was snowing that morning . . . Just fancy, snowing in the centre of Florence, and in March, too . . .'

The bus signalled and moved off. The boy had parked his broom and disappeared into the back of the trattoria. The first big logs had been put on to the fire where they roasted the meat and long flames were beginning to lick at them. Above the high building, blue woodsmoke drifted about uncertainly among the loose snowflakes, adding its sweet smell to the prevailing morning odours of coffee and exhaust fumes.

The Marshal looked at his watch. There was no time to do anything about the boy now if he was going to visit the prison as he wanted to. In any case it might be better to try talking to the lad himself first and leave the father out of it. And then it was more than likely that either or both of them would tell him to mind his own business. He sighed and made to cross the road. A car was coming along from his left and signalling intermittently in the face of the one-way traffic coming relentlessly towards it up Via Romana. Two girls were in the front and someone in the back was leaning forward between them, evidently trying to give directions from behind an enormous map.

More tourists. The invasion got earlier and earlier every year, making it impossible to go about normal business in the overcrowded narrow streets. Only the day before somebody had written to the editor of the *Nazione* suggesting ruefully that the mayor should provide a campsite somewhere out in the hills for the Florentines since there was no longer any room for them in their own city. However profitable tourism was supposed to be, they resented the annual invasion.

It was early, too, for the Sardinian bagpipers who didn't often appear between Christmas and Easter. But as the Marshal walked over towards Piazza Pitti and his Station he saw one coming towards him, enveloped in a long black shepherd's cloak, the white sheepskin airbag tucked under his arm. He was playing disjointedly and rather discordantly and no one took any notice of him or gave him any money. The Marshal automatically glanced across at the other side of the street expecting to see the second piper who played the melody on a small, oboe-like pipe, but he was nowhere in sight. Probably gone into one of the shops to beg. There was no time to linger and the Marshal went up the sloping forecourt of the Pitti Palace, squeezing his decidedly overweight bulk between the closely parked cars, and disappearing under the stone archway on the left.

When he poked his head into the office to say that he was taking the van he added, as an afterthought: 'It's snowing . . .'

Just outside Florence in the Chianti hills it snowed harder and the sky remained low and white all day. The loose flakes melted quickly on the stony, ochre-coloured roads but managed to cling to the newly sprouting wheat. The stiff little leaves on the olive trees each held a wafer of snow. There was no frost and evidently no danger of it, and the country people looking out of the barred windows of castles, villas and farmhouses regarded this unexpected but harmless weather with scant interest, only remarking with a doubtful look at the pale sky:

'It's rain we need . . .'

But the snow went on falling throughout the day. In the early evening it turned to sleet and by midnight it was raining hard, filling dark ditches, furrows and potholes and rinsing the small trees free of their burden. At four in the morning the lights of a van shone through the heavy rain, illuminating a stretch of the unmade road that connected the hilltop villages of Taverna and Pontino. The van stopped and its lights went out for a few moments before it backed up, turned and drove away showing blurred red tail-lights.

When the noise of the engine died away, slurred footsteps could be heard moving forward in the darkness. When they passed the gate of a farmhouse a dog began to bark but no light went on. The dog lost interest as the steps faded into the distance. At a bend in the road, marking the beginning of Pontino, an icon was framed by a little stone arch. Only the pinpoint of red light and the plastic flowers in a jamjar at its feet were visible. When the footsteps reached the icon they stopped. The tiny red lamp gave off a faint pink light which showed the slight form of a girl who reached out a hand towards the icon and then collapsed, hitting her forehead on one of the jutting stones of its arch. For over an hour the rain beat heavily on the grass, the arch and the crumpled figure, then the girl got to her feet and stumbled on towards the village of Pontino, sometimes wandering off the road, confused by more little red lights that appeared all around her. In the piazza there was one window lit but the girl, instead of making for the light, walked round in circles bumping into trees, benches and lamp posts in the darkness. It was only after some time, and then by accident, that she found herself looking in at the lighted window.

The rain beat on her head and swilled down the glass beyond which she saw a blur of flowers. In the middle of the flowers sat a gnome-like figure wearing a large green apron and a striped turban. He was rocking to and fro, apparently crooning to himself while dipping a long wooden painting brush into big pots of brightly coloured paint.

He daubed the paint on to the white daisies in his lap, turning them turquoise, magenta and blue.

Above the daubing figure was a tiny red light and a plaster figure of the Virgin dandling a chipped baby. The flowers in the vase at the foot of the statue were plastic. The painted face of the Virgin stared out of the window with a faint smile as the girl lifted a wet cold hand to tap at the glass.

CHAPTER 2

'Ring Pisa first for helicopters, I want the car found. They'll need to start around the Via Senese at this end and work south—no, there's no point in road blocks by this time, it's too late . . . sometime yesterday morning, I've nothing more definite. I'll need dog-handlers immediately and they'll have to be sent out to Pontino, there's no need for them to check in here first—the girl they released is in shock. I'll have her brought down here to Florence as soon as she can be moved but we'll have to leave her where she is for the moment—in fact, put me through to Pontino again now, will you? They might have something more for me by now . . .'

There was a clean notepad lying on the desk before Captain Maestrangelo, and he held a pen in his hand but he made no notes. There was no need to. The routine at this stage never varied. It was unlikely that he would find it necessary to leave his office until the time came to visit the missing girl's parents and in the meantime he was capable of giving the usual orders while half asleep—which he very nearly was, having been called from his bed not much after five in the morning. It was now five twenty-five and he rubbed a hand over his unshaven face as he hung up and leaned back in his chair for a moment until the call from Pontino should come through. The lights were on in the office from which he commanded the Carabinieri Company covering the section of the city that lay south of the river Arno and a large tract of country going south through the Chianti hills to the borders of the Province of Siena. It was just his bad luck that the village of Pontino lay just within that border and that it was he, and not some Sienese colleague who had been awakened at dawn. The city outside his window was still invisible except for a barely discernible outline of the roofs of Borgo Ognissanti against the paler darkness of the sky. It was still raining but less heavily. The occasional small truck rumbled along the riverside going towards the central market. In half an hour a dozen or so cars would drive into the inner courtyard and the morning shift would take over. The routine never varied . . . road blocks if the kidnapping was reported immediately, helicopters, dogs, inform the Substitute Prosecutor, set up the search for the base-man, the wait for the first communication. The parents were the only variable and even they didn't vary much; their reactions followed a predictable pattern as well understood by the police as it was by the kidnappers. The Captain's call from Pontino came through. The Carabinieri Brigadier out in Pontino was now ready with a completed preliminary report which he read slowly, word for word as he had written it, meticulous and too long. The Captain didn't interrupt him. No Substitute Prosecutor would appreciate being called at this hour.

'*The girl then said*, *in very approximate Italian*, ''*They've still got Deborah. I have to call the American Consulate.'' She later became much less coherent. I then telephoned the local doctor and Headquarters . . .'*

The only thing bothering the Captain at this stage was the sort of Substitute Prosecutor he would get. These cases were lengthy and delicate. It wasn't just that the parents had to be kept under control despite the fact that they and the police were in many respects working at cross purposes, it was the danger of some third party interfering . . . a go-between with power and influence was what the Captain dreaded most . . .

'A woollen sweater, blue with red and darker blue pattern across the shoulders. One pair of blue jeans, faded, American label, in the pockets of which were found two cinema tickets, one wallet, brown leather with a red painted design, containing . . .'

An experienced Substitute Prosecutor who would stand by him if things got tricky . . . and he hadn't always been lucky . . .

'Throat lozenges labelled ''Winky'', made in Milan, the paper torn and three of the lozenges remaining. A folded letter hand-written in English on lined exercise paper and addressed to the American Consul General of Florence, no envelope—'

'What!'

'There was no envelope—'

'The letter, Brigadier, the letter! The contents?'

'I'm afraid there's nobody here who can . . .'

'I'm coming out there immediately.' Well, whoever the Substitute turned out to be, he was going to be got out of bed at quarter to six whether he liked it or not. It wasn't the best foot to start off on but there it was . . .

The Substitute was a new man, Milanese, judging by the rapidity of his speech and the way he mumbled his S's, and far from being annoyed, he seemed to be amused.

'I was just asking myself whether it was worth while going to bed or not. I'll take a shower and be with you in twenty minutes—I trust you've had plenty of experience in this sort of thing?'

'Yes.'

'Good. I haven't. I'll take that shower.' And he rang off.

Nonplussed, the Captain ordered a car and, after a moment's thought, told his sleepy adjutant that he was going back to his quarters to shave and have a coffee.

Asking himself whether there was any point in going to bed . . .? What sort of man . . . this letter business didn't ring true at all . . . that they had taken the two girls and released one could simply mean a problem of identification, although even that was unlikely, but to send a first message before the parents had time to become frantic, possibly before they even knew . . . the whole thing could be a hoax, and yet the girl's condition . . . a hoax gone wrong! Impossible to judge anyway without reading the thing when they got out there . . . whether it was worthwhile going to bed at five-forty-five in the morning? What sort of Substitute Prosecutor was this going to be?

One who smoked too much, that was evident by the time the car turned on to the autostrada going south towards Siena, its light and siren going although the roads were fairly quiet. It was still dark and the weather was wet and foggy, but the blue fog inside the car was worse as the Substitute lit his third pungent little Tuscan cigar. The Captain tried to slide the back window down as unobtrusively as possible when the young Sub-lieutenant sitting beside the driver began to choke. But the Substitute caught his movement and, with a quick sidelong smile and a rueful glance at the offending object, he leaned back in his seat and said solemnly: 'It's my only vice.'

Out of the corner of his eye the Captain took in the man's elegant, obviously expensive clothes, noted the perfume not quite smothered by cigar smoke, and remembered the remark about whether it was worth while going to bed. He said nothing.

The car left the autostrada and the bright new factories dotted about the valley and took a narrow, winding road up into the hills on the right. Even in the dreary beginnings of a rainy dawn the newly sprouting vines dotted the hillside with a green that was almost luminous, but the olive trees were the same ghostly grey as the fog. A few people were already astir in the first village they passed through, and when they reached the piazza in Pontino higher up a huddled group stood within the light and warmth of the doorway of the Bar Italia waiting for the first bus down to Florence. The baker and the newsagent were open and there was a light on in the Carabinieri station that stood between them. An anxious young face disappeared from the window as their car drew up and parked under the dripping trees, but it was the Brigadier himself who appeared at the door to meet them. He looked harassed and he was. He hadn't expected this precipitate visit and in the last hour he had bawled out everyone in sight. Whoever had washed up last night hadn't cleaned the cooker, there was no light-bulb in the one cell in the basement and someone had had to be dispatched to wake up the ironmonger because nobody could find a spare. The coffee made by that blasted mother's boy Sartini had been like water as usual and the Brigadier himself hadn't had time to go home and shave. One of his men had been foolish enough to point out that the Company Captain was unlikely to want to use the cooker and that there hadn't been anybody in that cell in all the eight years he'd been there. The Brigadier had still been bawling him out when Sartini had spotted the car.

'Captain.' The Brigadier saluted the Substitute and Captain and the young lieutenant, and stepped back to let them in. The driver waited in the car. 'I'm afraid everything's not as I would like it to be here—you know, of course that we've been without a Marshal for two months now—not that I can't cope after twenty years service in this village, but even so—'

'Twenty years . . . then you know this area inside out.'

'Every blade of grass. That's not what I—'

'Good. The girl? Is she conscious?' The Captain sat down in the Brigadier's chair where the girl's effects were neatly folded and labelled. He immediately took up and unfolded the piece of lined paper. The Substitute had refused the chair offered to him, choosing instead to wander about the room, taking brief puffs on his cigar and regarding everything and everyone with an amused detachment that gave the impression of his being mildly surprised but pleased at having to perform the office of Public Prosecutor. He settled by the window and stared across at the red brick Communist club beyond the budding trees.

'She's in the cottage hospital, still unconscious as far as I know—I've left one of my boys there in case she comes to, but she's running a high temperature and they're afraid of bronchial pneumonia. We've no way of knowing how long she was out in that rain. She's wounded, too, in one leg, but she can't be moved down to Florence until twenty-four hours have passed because she cracked her head when she fell and there could be concussion.'

'Lieutenant.' The Captain passed the note up to the young officer standing stiffly just inside the door. The Captain's own English was passable but the younger man's was fluent. He read the letter aloud:

Dear Daddy,

They've kidnapped me. Please help me. They will send a message to the Consulate. You have to help me, Daddy, I need you.

Debbie

The Captain stared before him in silence for some time.

'That's all there is, sir.' The young Lieutenant handed back the letter. The Captain took it and looked at it, still without speaking. Finally he said: 'Thank you. Go over to the hospital and relieve the local man. Sit by this other girl's bed. Her name' he picked up the Brigadier's report from beside the telephone 'is Katrine, Katrine . . . If she comes round, talk to her. Write down anything that she says, even in her sleep or in fever. You'll have to stay even through the night, if necessary. We don't know what nationality she is but since her Italian is poor it's likely that she spoke English with her American friend. Get over there immediately. Can you spare a man, Brigadier, to show him the way?'

'Yessir. Sartini!' The Brigadier went off in search of 'that blasted mother's boy', pleased with the thought of being rid of him, even for twenty minutes.

The Substitute had turned from the window and was watching the Captain curiously A typewriter was clacking disjointedly in the next room.

'Something odd?'

'It seems so. But then, it's too early to judge. We'll go on with routine procedure for now.'

'Which is?'

'Dog-handlers will be here shortly. With the girl's clothes we should be able to trace her back at least to the point at which she was dropped during the night—or I hope so, after all that rain. In the meantime, the helicopters will patrol the surrounding area, especially where there are empty farmhouses or huts—the Brigadier here will know every possible hiding-place. Normally I'd also put out road blocks but in this case it's already too late.'

'Isn't it possible, though, that the other girl could be a hundred kilometres from here and that this one was dumped here to put you off the scent?'

'It's more than possible, it's probable, but until we know where else to look we'll look here. The real search can't begin until we find out what sort of kidnappers we're dealing with. For the moment—for all we know—they could be a couple of amateurs from this village who've got the girl hidden ten minutes from here. So we search here. And at least we'll find the girls' car because according to what one can make out of her statement, they were removed from it somewhere on the road between here and Taverna yesterday morning . . .'

A commotion outside the window announced the arrival of the van with the dogs and their handlers. A small crowd had gathered in the piazza as the morning advanced and people came out to buy bread or eat a hurried breakfast in the bar before catching the bus. One or two of the cars parked beneath the trees in the centre started up and moved off. The dogs were restless and panting, their breath steamy in the rain. One of the handlers came into the office and saluted briefly.

'Captain. What have you got for us?'

From the heap of clothing he took the girl's blue jeans, grumbling, 'After that downpour last night . . .'

As soon as the handler had left, the Brigadier poked his head round the door.

'I've kept the florist here in case you wanted to talk to him. Otherwise I'll let him get back to work. I've had his statement typed up.'

The clacking in the next room had stopped.

'I'll see him. Bring his statement in, too.'

The florist had removed his big green apron but the Brigadier had to force him to take off his trilby as he brought him in the door, muttering under his breath, 'This is a State office, you know very well . . .'

The florist sat down, his back straight, his hat gripped tightly on his knees, mortified at having to exhibit his bald crown, a thing he never did, even at mealtimes. He uncovered his head only after switching out the light at bedtime.

The Captain glanced at him and said quickly: 'Cavalry?'

The old man, who had been about to start grumbling about being kept so long from his work, blushed with pride and pleasure. 'Second Genova.'

He kept a photograph of himself on horseback in full dress uniform in the back of the shop. In those days he'd had thick wavy hair. There wasn't a girl in the village he couldn't . . . but when he thought about it, there was nothing in his statement, so far as he could remember, that said anything about . . . He tried to read it again, upside down, but the Captain picked it up, murmuring as he glanced through it: 'It's obvious from the way you sit. Something you never lose . . .'

MORI, Vittorio, born in Pontino, Province of Florence, 11.3.1913 and presently resident there. Occupation: florist

A.Q.: Towards five-thirty this morning, having just got back from the flower market, I was working in the front quarters of my shop when I got the idea I'd heard a funny noise just outside the window . . .

'Got the idea you heard?' The Captain looked up, puzzled.

'Well, because, in the first place I had the radio on, and what with the paraffin stove going—that makes a bit of noise—and a towel round my head . . . I was trying to get my hair and clothes dry. I'd got soaked going to the market.'

The Captain couldn't avoid a swift glance at the shiny dome flanked by two tufts of grey hair.

The florist twisted his hat round unhappily. 'At my age you have to take care of yourself . . . Anyway, that was the other thing, it was raining so hard, rattling at the windowpane in the dark . . . even so, I was convinced I'd heard something, and at that hour there's nobody else up except the baker, and he's over here on this side of the

Piazza, so I got up to take a look and saw this girl lying there in the rain. It gave me a fright, I don't mind telling you. She's not from round here . . .?'

'No.' The Captain volunteered no information.

'I thought not. I went straight round to the Brigadier's house and rang. I didn't want to touch her, not knowing what . . . but I did put a blanket over her. The Brigadier got one of his men and we carried her over here between us. She came to for a bit when we brought her into the light, but I had difficulty following what she said. I gather she's foreign . . .'

'Go on.'

'Nothing much else, really, as you can see from what I told the Brigadier—except that, whatever's happened, I've got nothing to do with it—I expect she was attracted by the light in my window if she was lost.'

'I expect so.'

'The baker works in the back, you see, so he doesn't show a light until he opens at six. Anyway, it's nothing to do with me. I've told you all I know and I ought to be getting back—I've lost two hours of work as it is.'

'Have you read through your statement?'

'With the Brigadier, before.'

'And you don't want to add or change anything?'

'I've told you everything, it's nothing to do with . . .'

'Then sign here.'

The thick fingers were spattered with blobs of bright paint.

'And here . . . Right, you can go. If we need you again we'll send for you, but it's not likely.'

The florist's hat was back in place before the door had closed behind him. The Captain called back the guard who had shown him out; 'Ask the Brigadier to come in, will you?'

The Brigadier was red in the face: 'Things aren't as they should be . . .' he began again, and tailed off as the

Captain indicated that he should sit down.

The Substitute suddenly pulled up a chair, lit a large pipe, and began watching with interest as the other two examined the girl's effects.

'Not a thing that helps us,' said the Captain at last. 'And we haven't even got her surname.'

'Just her first name. She wasn't very coherent . . . and she was in such a bad state I couldn't force her . . .'

'No, no, I realize that.'

'The main problem was that she was obsessed with the idea of telephoning—in fact, she's still got the token in her hand, we couldn't get her to part with it.'

'But she didn't mention this letter?'

'Not once.'

The Captain examined it again, frowning. 'Then she was told not to. Not yet, at any rate. Just to make the telephone call. Well, we'll have to wait until we can talk to her. We might give the hospital a call, I think, and get the latest report. If there's any likelihood of her regaining consciousness during the day, it will be worthwhile waiting here.'

The girl hadn't regained consciousness. There were screens around her bed, and beside it sat the young Sub-lieutenant, almost as motionless as the form under the sheets, staring earnestly at the bandaged head and the small white face.

CHAPTER 3

They drove back down to Florence, the Captain silent and thoughtful, the Substitute smoking, making the occasional rapid remark, watching the passing of the wet, ploughed soil between rows of vines and the tops of umbrella pines appearing out of the misty valley far below, smoking . . .

It had stopped raining by the time they drew into the courtyard at Headquarters. The Substitute jumped out, saying he had to be in court in ten minutes, hurried round to shake the Captain's hand through the car window, and said eagerly: 'Have lunch with me. I want to know all about kidnappings. I'd already heard that you're an expert.'

'Of necessity. In this area . . .'

'I'll pick you up at one.'

'But . . . you haven't a car . . .?'

'Never use it—unless my registrar drives. Driving interferes with my smoking. I'll get your sentry room to call me a taxi.' And he was gone, a trenchmac thrown round his shoulders, hurrying across the yard and along the old cloister that led to the exit, leaving behind him a trail of aromatic blue smoke.

Captain Maestrangelo went upstairs to his office and sat down, rubbing a hand wearily over his face. He knew from long experience that a kidnapping usually meant the involvement of the Sardinian shepherds who had, over the past twenty years or so, been steadily leaving their island and bringing their flocks to graze on the hills around Florence. They kept themselves to themselves, never mixing with the Florentines, who admired their cheesemaking and were outraged by their kidnapping. The Sardinians were great experts in both activities for which their remote dwellings surrounded by rich Tuscan pastures were the ideal environment. The Captain sent his Adjutant for the Sardinian file and then set about selecting a group of his most experienced men.

'Calaresu, Giovanni?'

'He's inside.'

'That wouldn't stop him—check up on whether any of

his cell-mates have been released lately. Where's his wife?'

'Gone back to her mother in Sardinia with the children—he's in for eight years.'

'Find out if he's had any visitors.'

'Demontis, Salvatore. He could be our man—he lives near Pontino.'

'Could be, but remember we don't know where these girls live. Take a look round there, in any case. Next.'

'The adjutant opened the next folder from the pile on the Captain's desk.

'Mundula, Mario.'

'I don't know him.'

'No convictions, sir. They've been here since the fifties, no children, his brother lives with them. They own their two farms and between four and five hundred sheep. Pretty well off.'

They put the file aside.

The Captain kept a file on the whole of the Sardinian community in Tuscany. So many of them were interrelated or came from the same Sardinian village that all of them, with or without a record, could usually tell him something if they would. Unless forced, they wouldn't. Unless forced, they were the most stubbornly silent people in the world. Silent out of pride and independence, not out of fear. The Captain, despite the amount of work and trouble they caused him, liked the Sardinians.

'Piladu, Paolo?'

'He's all right, but his eldest boy's been in trouble once or twice . . . pay them a visit and see what the boy's doing now, if he's got any work. He's never been much help to his father.'

They worked on through the files for the rest of the morning, a routine they had been through so often that they commented mostly in half-sentences or barely audible grunts. By twenty to one they had finished. The Captain glanced at his watch. These men should have gone off duty at twelve but he was able to dismiss only two of them whom he could replace with experienced men from the afternoon shift. These two, when they arrived, he sent to the prison. The others went off to have a bite to eat before begining their checks on the Sardinian shepherds they had picked out. When they had all left, the Adjutant removed the unwanted files and the Captain sat back in his chair, musing. Outside the window it was raining again, harder than ever. Both helicopter pilots and dog-handlers would be cursing the weather. Each time there was a pause in his routine and he had time to think, the Captain was reminded that there were a good many things about this case that didn't ring true. Yet he felt more relaxed and confident than was usual at this stage and he couldn't help asking himself why. It was only on glancing again at his watch at three minutes to one and wondering what time the Substitute would turn up that he realized that the Substitute was the reason why. Instead of directing the inquiry he had admitted his inexperience and was following it. The Captain was freer than he could ever remember being in his whole career. What was more, the Substitute gave the impression that he could cope with any third party interference, at any level, with nothing more than the pursed lips and flicker of amusement with which he seemed to regard everything that went on around him. He had even introduced himself—'Fusarri, Virgilio Fusarri'—with an eager, boyish air that matched his thin face and figure but belied his hair which was grey. He must be forty. It's either money, thought the Captain, he doesn't need to work, or else it's a way of disarming people. He has the air of someone who always gets his own way. Well, it was convenient to be able to handle a case without interference from the magistracy, but it was also irregular. Captain Maestrangelo had no taste for the irregular. He picked up his telephone and got the radio room.

'I want to know about any girls reported missing since yesterday. Message to all stations.'

'In Tuscany?'

'Yes . . . No, throughout the country. Relay it to General Command.' As soon as he put the phone down it rang:

'Sentry room here, sir. Substitute Prosecutor asking for you.'

It was one o'clock precisely.

'Tell him I'll be down immediately.'

One o'clock precisely. 'A real northerner, then,' muttered the Captain as he switched off his desk lamp. 'But they overdo it.'

'Oh! Let's not overdo it!' Fusarri opened an accusing hand at the restaurant owner who was wheeling up a trolley laden with fifteen different hors d'oeuvres. 'You know I can't touch this stuff with the liver I've got—and I barely eat at lunchtime.'

'Then it's time you changed restaurants,' retorted the Florentine owner, evidently considering this an unlikely eventuality.

'Give me a bit of that stuff there.' The cigar waved in the general direction of half a dozen kinds of salami and some boletus mushrooms. 'Serve the Captain—what's this stuff you've given me? What is it?'

'Crostini. Florentine pâté. Homemade.'

'No, no, no. Give it to the Captain, he's Florentine. I can't eat it.' He flicked open the attaché case on the chair beside him. The left side contained neatly arranged papers, the right contained stacks and rows of pipes, tobacco tins, cigarettes and cigars and a large selection of tablets and capsules. He chose four different coloured capsules and tucked them discreetly beneath his plate.

'Liver,' he explained. 'It's these things that do it.' He looked accusingly at the cigar between his slim fingers, stubbed it out quickly and attacked the salami which, in the Captain's opinion, couldn't be the ideal food for a bad liver, but the expected complaint didn't come. The accusations seemed to be fairly random. The Captain got on with his crostini which were excellent. This wasn't a restaurant he could afford to eat in and he was enjoying himself.

'Well then.' Fusarri whipped his plate to one side, swallowed a red capsule and selected a fresh packet of cigarettes from his case. 'Tell me about kidnapping.'

'You've never had a case before?'

'Can you imagine?' He snapped his lighter, 'I've only been down here six months. Before that, five years in the Alto Adige practising my German. Every problem but. Tuscan speciality, it seems, like that stuff you're eating. I apologize; I tend to eat too fast—you can't imagine what it does to my liver.'

'More of a Sardinian speciality, to be precise. In this area, at least.'

'Why Tuscany?'

'Two reasons: first, because they moved here, the Sardinians, to find pasture when the land they had grazed for centuries was taken from them for development—the Costa Smeralda, etcetera. They were forced into a system of apartheid, driven off the good grazing land up into the mountains. It happened just at the time when the Tuscan peasants were abandoning their land to go and work in the factories. Those Sardinians who had any money at all were able to buy up land for practically nothing and get rich pasture for their sheep. They do very nicely.'

'So what's the problem?'

'The ones who came later and are still arriving all the time. They're fairly poor—in any case, land here costs a fortune now. The easy days are long gone. These shepherds live wild, most of them on the same mountain just outside Florence, in abandoned houses which often have no light or running water. Their families, if they come over too, live down below on the edge of the city in a sort of ghetto. It's usually a case of one shepherd and his meagre flock having to support a wife, God knows how many children, plus brothers and sisters and aged relatives. Don't get me wrong—sheep are profitable, very profitable, but if it's cheeses you rear them for then one man can only deal with a few. The trouble is their sons don't want to know; they're not prepared to live that sort of life but they can't find other work. The result is that they hang around the city and most family incomes are supplemented by crime of one sort or another. The other result is a lot of prejudice against them in the city. People only see the good-for-nothing sons who hang around bars getting into fights and pushing drugs; they don't see the real shepherd, the man who spends almost all of his life alone, spends his days making the cheeses they take for granted and his nights sleeping sometimes only for a couple of hours because it's lambing time.'

'You like them?' There was no hint of irony in the Substitute's voice.

'Yes. And I respect them. They're a proud race. Disinherited.'

'What's the other reason for Tuscany being rife with kidnappings? You said there were two.'

'Our Sardinian colleagues. They know their job, they know their people and they know their territory. There isn't a spot left on the island of Sardinia where they can hide a victim, despite the difficult and practically inaccessible terrain. Five years ago there were over two hundred kidnappings there—the pickings were rich along the Costa Smeralda for those who were sticking it out on the hills above—but last year there were only three, and one of those a complete failure. So the big organizers have moved here. Tuscany's full of rich residents, Italian and foreign, and there's no shortage of recruits among the poorer shepherds and their families.'

'You discount any other suspects?'

'No. I just look for the obvious first.'

'Mm. Oh! Cesare!'

'I'll be right with you!'

'I suppose we'd better eat something.'

They ate pasta, the Substitute continuing to ask rapid questions while winding rapid forkfuls, his eyes always fixed on the Captain's.

'What happens next?'

'We're looking for the base-man, the person who suggested the victim. It has to be somebody who knows, is connected with or in a position to observe the victim and the family.'

'And what do we know about the family?'

'Nothing as yet, as I'm sure you've realized. We need the information the injured girl can give us when she comes round. The surname, and the message she was to telephone—it's very abnormal indeed for any personal message from the victim to be sent so soon. There's usually just a ransom demand and then a longish gap to put the parents in a panic.'

'And we don't seem to have any parents.'

'Exactly. What's really worrying me is that we may be dealing with amateurs.'

'Worries you? Surely that would make your job easier?'

'If you mean we'll catch them, yes it will, but it will also, almost certainly, mean the girl's death. Amateurs are incompetent, and then they panic. Professionals are well organized, never seen by their victims, and they don't kill. It's bad for business. If people weren't sure of getting the victim for their money they wouldn't be so willing to pay up. With amateurs there's no point in paying, they're likely to kill the victim off anyway, out of fear. I'd rather deal with professionals.'

'But how can you get panic-stricken parents to understand the difference and cooperate with you?'

'It's my job,' said the Captain quietly.

The Substitute looked at him closely. There was no doubt that the Captain radiated calm and confident seriousness. The parents would cooperate all right, so long as nobody else interfered. The Substitute made up his mind that nobody would be allowed to interfere.

'Do you think the family might be here on holiday?'

'It's possible. Especially if they have a villa and come every year. If it's a professional job they will have been observed over a long period and their habits and financial status will be known.'

'Ah . . .!' This exclamation was directed not at the Captain but at the aromatic roast loin of pork that was steaming towards them, propelled by Cesare.

'Serve the Captain first—and don't give me any, you know it's bad for me, not more than a taste, one slice—that's enough! How anyone can eat all this stuff at lunchtime I'll never know!'

When Captain Maestrangelo got back to his office he realized he had eaten far too much too quickly in an effort to keep up with the Substitute. The latter had vanished as punctually as he had appeared. 'Due in court at two-thirty—have to run—Cesare! call me a taxi! I'll give you a lift back. You will telephone me if there's any news? Here . . . between eight and eight-thirty at this number.'

Watching the traffic and the rain swallow up the departing taxi, the Captain wondered how the man stayed so thin if he ate that way every day. Must take a lot of exercise, was his conclusion, and he turned his mind to more important matters. On his desk there was a message from the Sub-lieutenant at the hospital. The girl had not regained consciousness and she had a very high fever. He would stay on through the night although the local doctor had said it was probably useless.

By three-thirty it was raining so pitilessly that the sky had turned black and all the street lights were on. The helicopter pilots reported in by radio. They were coming in. They could see absolutely nothing and were wasting time and fuel. The dog-handlers struggled on for another hour but then they, too, gave up. The Alsatians, their thick pelts soaked and steaming, had sniffed with some certainty around a little icon of the Virgin which stood by the roadside, sheltered from the rain by a stone arch, but after that they had rambled unhappily this way and that and returned whining to their handlers, who were knee-deep in mud, soaked to the skin and cursing roundly.

The Captain waited, dealing patiently with the routine paperwork with which he was constantly burdened, and diplomatically with an influential gentleman who wanted an impossible favour to do with the son's military service.

The patrols searching the first group of farms around the village of Pontino were the only ones to bring the Captain anything when they returned, muddy and exhausted, after their double shift. They tipped on to his desk their haul of three shotguns and a pistol for which the respective owners had no licences, and one dose of heroin. They also reported other stolen goods which they found but left to be collected later: a stolen Fiat 500, eight sheep and a donkey.

The Captain telephoned the American Consulate.

CHAPTER 4

'A case for galoshes,' remarked the Substitute, tossing a cigar end out of the jeep and looking around at the steam rising slowly from the wet earth. The sky above them was blue, the air sweet and the spring sunshine warm.

The Brigadier and the Captain sank their cavalry boots deep into the clay soil and began looking about. The Substitute dodged from stone to stone until he gained the hardened ground in front of the farmhouse where stone steps led sideways up to the front door. He ran up the steps and knocked but no one answered.

Hens and geese were picking around in two small haystacks and fleets of tiny yellow chickens were half hidden beneath some planking and under the foundations of some rickety sheds. The boggy sheepfold was empty. Strands of wool fringed all its fencing. On the glistening horizon two black dots appeared, separated, and became helicopters roaring low overhead and scattering the distracted fowl. The Substitute knocked again smartly, but the Brigadier appeared in the doorway of the stable and called up: 'There'll be nobody in the house at this hour!'

'Well then?' What on earth were they here for?

The Brigadier set down a fat puppy that he had been holding and squelched towards the yard, driving a dozen pullets before him.

'I'd hoped he'd still be grazing that pasture there.' He waved an arm at an empty green field with mist rising from the cropped grass. 'He was last year about now but Easter's late, I hadn't thought on, and he'll not move down until Palm Sunday like as not, and if he's still over on the mountain he'll be up Three Valleys Pass and that's an hour and a half of a walk for him, going as the crow flies, but longer for us in the jeep because there's no direct road—and then to get at him we'd have to take a cart track that'll be more like a river bed after yesterday's rain. The thing is, he'll likely not move till Palm Sunday, I should have thought on—we'll take the old road over to Demontis's farm and come back here at six this evening when Piladu will be milking. His wife'll be back then which is just as well—she cleans for the factor's wife over at "Il Cantuccio" in the mornings. We'll get on over to see Demontis. I should have thought on about Easter being late.'

'Ah.' The Substitute accepted this jumble of incomprehensible information equitably. 'Every blade of grass,' the man had said, and he evidently meant it. They climbed back into the jeep and went on along the rutted lane, lurching and splashing through deep puddles, the Brigadier worrying audibly all the way because 'things weren't as they should be.' This remark did not, as his passengers might have thought, refer either to the condition of the road or to his not having thought on about Easter, but to the problem of where the other two were going to eat lunch. He hoped fervently that they would go back to Florence and had dropped several hints in the hope of getting this information out of them, but the Captain was always concentrating on the job in hand as if nothing else mattered and the magistrate only smiled and nodded distractedly, his mind apparently elsewhere.

Outside the Demontis farm a little dog shot out of a barrel and came to be petted by the Brigadier. A short round woman in a big flowered apron, her long grey-black pigtail wound into a thick bun, came out of her cheese room and sent the Captain and the Brigadier along the edge of a muddy, sprouting cornfield to a distant pasture, leaving the Substitute to keep his shoes dry near the farmhouse. They couldn't see the shepherd until they crossed the last rise but they could hear the sheepbells on the clear air. The shepherd was on his feet, jacket slung over his shoulder, gazing skywards, his cap pulled low to shade his eyes. He was watching the circling helicopters.

'What are they looking for?' he asked them without any preliminary greeting.

'We thought you might tell us.'

He told them nothing. The three men stood together for some time while the long-faced sheep ambled around them, sometimes coming close to examine them but scuttering away at the slightest of their movements, sending a ripple of bells through the whole flock.

The Captain had no illusions about being able to guess what Demontis knew or didn't know. The old shepherd's face was lined and brown. His deep-set eyes roved slowly over his flock, over them, over his flock again, with no change in his expression. He might have been watching over all of them for a century. There was no infecting him with their urgency. The newpaper sticking out of his jacket pocket carried last Sunday's date.

'If you hear anything . . .'

If he heard anything he would not dream of doing anything about it but would go on gazing indifferently over the heads of his sheep. They left him looking up at the sky again. He didn't turn his head to look after them and he was so still that even at a short distance they could no longer distinguish him from his surroundings.

When they got back to the farmyard the Substitute had vanished. They could hear his rapid speech and then the fat shepherdess's delighted scream of laughter. They appeared in the doorway of the house, the woman red in the face and still chuckling. The Substitute said goodbye to her and ran lightly to the jeep carrying a polythene bag.

'Ricotta,' he explained, opening the bag for them to inspect the fluffy white mound with the whey still running out of the cheese paper.

'The lady informs me,' said the Substitute as they drove away and the Captain reported the husband's silence, 'that his brother is a bad lot, the bane of her life, that she would never have married Salvatore—who, I should tell you, is a saint, a veritable saint, when considered on his own—if she had known she'd be stuck with the terrible Antonio as well. Among his worst crimes are not being married, not turning up at milking times and stealing food.'

'I know,' the Brigadier said, 'Especially as he bets. He's not above stealing a few of her mature cheeses and selling them. They're worth quite a bit of money.'

'Yes . . . but recently he's been stealing other things from the house, too . . .'

'He has?' The Captain looked up.

'Yes. I thought you might be interested.'

'I am. We'd better stay away from here for the moment.'

'You think so?'

'If he turns out to be a feeder for the kidnappers,' explained the Captain, 'he'd be too easy to replace if we showed any interest in him.'

'And if we leave him alone he'll lead us somewhere.'

'Not far, I'm afraid. Feeders are small fry, though they're well paid if the ransom's high. There will be at least two of them, but even if they know each other they won't know anybody else except the one man who took them on and will eventually pay them. Meantime they're given money to buy food.'

'But the person they pass the food to . . .'

'Will be one of those guarding the victim, but they may never meet. The food is often left in a given place and collected later. The only man who knows everyone concerned is the base-man.'

'In that case we surely are talking about professionals, despite your doubts earlier.'

'I still have doubts.' The Captain frowned. 'I still don't like that letter and I don't like the timing. It's only four months since I got one of the big boys from the Sardinian gang that operates here.'

'The Donati kidnapping. Yes, I remember. He was shot getting away with the ransom.'

'And two others got away by the skin of their teeth. I'd be surprised to hear they were still in the country, and if they are they should be lying low.'

The jeep was bouncing them about mercilessly as the Brigadier tried to get back to the village in time for the Captain and the Substitute to go back to Florence and eat.

'But if they're given money for the food . . .' the Substitute was trying vainly to put a bouncing lighter to his cigar.

'As his sister-in-law said, he's a bad lot. He's also stupid and thinks he's clever. He'll have been gambling the money away and then stealing the food from her.'

'Not just food.' He finally managed to light up as they reached the main road, and he blew a sidelong stream of blue smoke behind the Brigadier's head. 'There were other items . . . of a very personal nature that he couldn't be selling, if you see what I mean.'

'She really wants him put away, then . . .' The Captain wondered at this hatred which was stronger even than family loyalty.

'He may have other faults,' pointed out the Substitute, 'that she didn't care to mention. It's a lonely spot and the husband seems to be away all day with his sheep.'

'Mmm. Well, we'll have him watched but keep our distance. I have hopes of Piladu's telling us something this evening. He's got a stolen donkey to account for so we've got more leverage there.'

'And is there' the Substitute pursed his lips in a smile and drew on his cigar 'a brother in the case?'

'No, but there's a wife who won't be too pleased with her husband. There are two sons but the elder one's no good and won't work on the farm. If Piladu gets put away for stealing that donkey his wife will be left in a real mess.'

'Then we can offer to negotiate.'

'Quite. If you've no objections . . .?'

'None at all. I told you, I shall leave everything to you. Well, here we are. I'm beginning to get quite fond of this little piazza. What we need to know now is what the

Brigadier here is going to give us for lunch. After that I have to leave you and get back to Florence.' The Brigadier's red face began to sweat. 'We can start with my ricotta and a flask of good Chianti. What about sending one of your boys across to that overflowing grocer's there to get us a fine Tuscan loaf? I don't eat much at lunchtime myself but we must think of the Captain here who's doing all the work . . . perhaps a string or two of those wild boar sausages—do you think they're local? If they are we must sample them, be an insult not to. Well, Brigadier?'

'Well?'

'Well, it must have wandered in here by mistake.'

'Wandered in . . . ? That donkey was stolen fifty kilometres away!'

'Must have fancied a walk—keep still, blast you! *Keep still!*' The milk sprayed into the bucket in a few short spurts and Piladu pushed the animal forward, let two heavily pregnant ewes push past him and reached out to grasp the wool of a lamb that was trying to jump the rail where the Captain and the Brigadier were leaning. 'Down, you bugger, down! Come here!' He pulled its hind legs towards him, turning on his stool to call to his younger son who was milking invisibly somewhere behind him, 'Leave her! Leave her for me, she's too tricky for you, I'll see to her! And shift that dog!'

The two hundred sheep jostled and complained and tried to jump the queue that stretched deep into an olive grove. The young dog, new to the job, ran about excitedly causing more confusion; the old one, who was an expert, was so very old that he continually rolled over and fell asleep. Every now and then Piladu turned and barked at him to encourage him. The Captain and the Brigadier were getting nowhere.

'That donkey has to be explained,' shouted the Brigadier over the racket of the baaing sheep and the barking man.

'Woof! Ruff! Get up, you lazy sod! You'd better have a talk to it, then. Let the ram through! Gianni! Let him through, he's causing havoc back there! Ho! Ho! Wake up, ruff ruff, Fido, blast you!'

Even so, Piladu knew that once milking was over the facts had to be faced, and faced in the kitchen where his wife would be listening. It was going dark by the time the shepherd and his son shed their ragged leather milking jackets and carried two buckets each up the stone steps to the kitchen, followed by the two carabinieri. Piladu's wife, peeling artichokes in the gloom at the kitchen table, put down her knife and accepted the milk without a word. The kitchen smelled of sour milk and woodsmoke.

'Do you mind if we sit down?' the Captain asked the woman. She nodded towards the far end of the table and then turned her back on them, pouring the milk into two big cauldrons by the fire. Two tiny children appeared from the shadows.

'When are we going to eat?'

'Get out, or else help with the artichokes.'

They got out.

The shepherd poured some wine from a tattered straw flask into four greasy tumblers and the men sat at the oil-cloth-covered table. The woman dropped rennet into the two cauldrons, stirred them, and then went on peeling the mound of artichokes in silence.

'Your eldest son's not here?' began the Brigadier.

'Him!' The shepherd drained his glass and reached for the flask. 'He's never here.' He had lost his cheekiness now that they were indoors and under the eye of his wife.

'Lucky you've got a good lad like this one, then.'

The second boy was a cheerful replica of his mother, his high, red cheeks almost burying his slanted dark eyes. He looked from one to the other of their faces but knew better than to open his mouth. The only sounds came from the other end of the room where the woman was splitting the artichokes and tossing them with a splash into a big plastic bowl. A big log settled in the fire with a shower of sparks and began to blaze fiercely, brightening the room and darkening its shadows.

'There's a girl missing.'

None of the family spoke or looked at the others. The woman, tight-lipped, turned her back on them and began to slap the milk vigorously with a peeled wand spiked at one end where smaller branches had been lopped off.

'Perhaps she's wandered here by mistake,' went on the Brigadier, determined to provoke an answer.

'You know better than that,' the shepherd mumbled.

'All right, I know better. We know all your tricks and kidnapping isn't one of them . . . The only thing is, we're not so sure about your son.'

Piladu slid a sidelong look at his wife's back. She had thrown the artichoke leaves into a bucket and turned to slap and stir the milk again.

Has he found work in Florence?' asked the Brigadier innocently.

'Florence!' Piladu spat the word, and then, as if to distract them, he snapped at his wife, 'when are we going to eat?'

'The woman said, more to herself than to him, 'How many things do you think I can do at once. Maria!'

A girl appeared from the next room. She couldn't have been more than thirteen or fourteen but her face was thickly painted and her clothes were frivolous, brightly coloured things. A long, glittering scarf was draped round her neck. She began setting out plates and glasses, walking round the two carabinieri as though they weren't there. Her cheap, strong perfume mingled with the sour milk and woodsmoke. When the table was ready she filled a deep pan with water and put it on the cooker, her movements slow and simpering in contrast to those of her mother, who quickly poured olive oil into a big black frying-pan, threw in the artichokes, covered them and rinsed her hands and arms before drawing a chair up to one of the cauldrons and sliding into the curd up to her elbows.

'That donkey,' insisted the Brigadier.

'I've told you—'

'It came here by mistake, yes. But there have been so many of these little mistakes, you see, that we've been obliged to have a warrant made out.'

'Here.' The woman didn't remove her arms from the curd, only nodded at her son and then at the bucket of peelings. He got up and went out to feed the rabbits. 'And you. Put the pasta on and get out.' All the time she was glowering at her husband, the look of fury in her narrow black eyes completely at odds with the gentle action of her arms as she gathered the curd towards herself slowly.

'We don't have to use this warrant, of course,' persisted the Brigadier quietly, and after a moment's pause he added: 'We found a dose of heroin over at Scano's place yesterday.'

It was possible, even in the flickering half-light, to see the shepherd's shoulders relax a little and then stiffen again.

'What do you want?'

'To know where it came from.' It was the Captain now who spoke.

'How should I know that?'

'Scano's boy is a friend of your son's. They go down to Florence together.'

'They don't bother to tell me where they're going.'

'No. But you could find out.'

'My son's not a drug addict.'

'How do you know?'

'What d'you mean?'

'How do you know he's not? Do you know what the

symptoms are? Have you ever looked at his arms? If your boy's on heroin he's not your son any longer. He belongs to the drug he's hooked on and he'll do anything to get it. Anything—'

'And I say he's not on any drugs. You didn't find that stuff here.'

'No. We found it over at Scano's. And Scano's son is a friend of your son's. Your son knows where it comes from even if he doesn't take the stuff himself. Even if he does, he's safe enough from us as long as he's not pushing. So you could help us.'

The shepherd stared down into his glass in silence, trying to spot the trap. His wife had finished gathering the curd and was wiping her hands on her apron. She went on preparing the supper, her body tense with listening as she tossed the artichokes, stirred the pasta and put half a dozen steaks to fry in another black iron pan. When she returned to the table and began scooping the first of the curd into a mould, they felt her eyes burning into them, all three of them. But still her hands moved in their own private world, turning and pressing the dripping white mound as though they were caressing a baby. Watching her face, the Brigadier said:

'We could ring you tomorrow. If you don't know now you could find out.'

But the shepherd was still trying to scent where the danger lay. Suddenly he said: 'What's all this got to do with a girl being missing?'

'Who said it had anything to do with that?'

'You mentioned it before.'

'We mentioned it, that's all. The only thing we want to know from you is where the stuff we found at Scano's came from.'

But the shepherd had smelt danger and was silent.

'We'll come back tomorrow,' said the Brigadier. 'If you can oblige us with that bit of information you can turn the donkey loose and we'll find it on the road for the man who reported it lost. If you can't help us we shall have to come back with that warrant.'

The Captain and the Brigadier got to their feet.

'Good night, Signora.' She didn't answer but went on turning and pressing, turning and pressing, her eyes bright with rage. Before they had crossed the yard her outburst began, and even the noisy engine of their jeep didn't drown her shrill fury.

'And I can't say I blame her,' remarked the Captain. It was after eight-thirty and in a few minutes the family would sit down to eat while she stood at the end of the table, still working. It would take her until at least eleven o'clock to deal with the pecorino, after which there was ricotta to be made from the boiled up second skimming. After that she would, no doubt, be too tired to eat anything. If her husband went to prison, leaving only the boy and herself to cope . . .'

'You said she goes cleaning, too?'

'Over at "Il Cantuccio", eleven to one, five mornings a week after the morning cheesemaking.'

'Good God . . .'

It was quite dark now as they bounced along the rough road. A red dot indicated the icon that marked the beginning of Pontino. A little further on dozens of similar dots appeared on the fronts of tightly-shuttered houses.

'You'd better drop me at the hospital.'

'Right you are, sir.'

'Have my car sent up in about fifteen minutes.'

From the hospital foyer he tried to telephone the Substitute who had been in court all afternoon and wanted to hear how things had gone. But there was no answer from the number he rang.

It took a little time to find the girl who had been moved and was not in the room that the Sub-lieutenant had told him how to find. With the help of a night nurse he found the right room and tiptoed in. There was an oxygen tent over the bed and in the dull light that was burning, the young officer's thin face looked deep pink.

'How is she?'

'She's had something of a relapse.' They were whispering. 'She was out of the oxygen tent earlier and her temperature was coming down with the antibiotics but then when she came to . . . she opened her eyes and suddenly seemed to go into a panic. She tried to get out of bed and had to be restrained.'

'She was delirious?'

'No, she was just terrified—perhaps, finding herself in bed in a strange place, she thought she was still captive.'

'A bit odd, even so. There was nothing in the room that might have frightened her? No one else was here?'

'Nothing. Nobody. The florist came up earlier but she was asleep, and he didn't even come into the room, just put his head round the door and left her some flowers; the night nurse has put them out in the corridor, I think . . .'

'And she hasn't said anything?'

'She sometimes calls for her friend and she's still worrying about the phone call she should have made. You can see . . .'

They leaned over the sleeping figure and saw through the polythene tent the hand on the counterpane closed in a tight fist.

'She still has the token. I've tried a few ways of getting it off her . . . offering to telephone for her and so on, thinking she might improve if that was off her mind . . .'

'I understand.'

'They say she'll sleep through the night. They gave her something . . .'

'Do you want to come back to Florence with me and get some sleep?'

'No, I'd rather stick it out. I can sleep a little here, if

necessary, but I want to be sure I'm here when she wakes up.'

'I'd like to know just what frightened her.' The Captain looked round the bare room, frowning. 'It couldn't have been you, I suppose?'

'No, sir. It couldn't have been me. She was looking the other way and didn't see me.'

CHAPTER 5

When she did see him it was without his knowing it. She hadn't moved or made a sound, just opened her eyes in the red-tinged darkness and seen him there without surprise as if she had been aware of his presence ever since he arrived. His head had fallen forward a little and his face was in shadow. She could see a sliver of white shirt, the braided collar of his black jacket, a star on his epaulette, the hand that rested along his crossed knee. Her eyes left him and examined the rest of the room. A loaded trolley had a white cloth that looked pink draped over it and an oxygen cylinder was just visible in a dark corner. The girl's eyes swivelled to the left and stared at the locker-top where the officer had left his hat, then to the right, watching him. He was trying to keep awake, forcing his eyelids open slightly every few minutes. Even so, he was asleep. Her eyes ran down the black jacket to where the man's watch was half hidden by a white cuff. Then her eyes closed again. For more than two hours their quiet breathing was the only sound in the small room.

The next time the girl opened her eyes the young officer was staring straight into them, his face strained and anxious. She asked him: 'What time is it?' as if they had been in the middle of a conversation.

'Three-thirty.'

'In the morning?'

'Yes.'

It was still dark and the red nightlight was still burning. A blustery wind was sending light flurries of rain against the window.

'I ought to call the nurse.'

'Not yet . . .' Her eyes moved to the left again to look at the locker. 'I don't want anybody to come. I'm so tired . . .'

'The doctor wanted you to sleep through the night.'

They were whispering for no reason except that the dim light and the sense of being awake when everyone else was asleep suggested it.

'I can go back to sleep.'

She spoke good English with only a trace of accent. The officer resisted the urge to take out a notebook, to ask questions. She seemed calm enough but the fit she had thrown on first wakening was fresh in his mind. The hospital staff wouldn't thank him for provoking another. Besides, any interrogation had to be left to the Captain, who had enough experience to separate the half-truths from the lies. The truth never came out until the fear wore off. So he sat still and let her talk, murmuring answers to the few questions she asked him, trying to memorize details that might be important. The hand lying on the white counterpane still clutched the telephone token but neither of them mentioned it. She talked in brief spurts in between which her eyes became glazed, probably as a result of whatever drug they had given her. Oddly enough, it was not during one of these silences but while she was talking that her eyes closed and her shallow breathing became deeper. He watched her closely for a long time but there was no further flicker of consciousness. Nevertheless, when he shifted noiselessly and settled back in his chair she spoke, apparently in her sleep, murmuring: 'You won't go away?'

'No.'

'Good . . .'

'Captain? I hope I haven't rung too early . . .'

'That's all right. Go on.'

'There isn't all that much because she soon fell asleep again but at least I've got their names. She's called Nilsen and she's Norwegian.'

'And the other girl?'

'Maxwell. Deborah Maxwell. They'll probably both have a police permit since they study Italian at the University.'

'They're registered as full-time students?'

'Not on a degree course but at the Cultural Centre for Foreigners where they've been going since last September.'

'And they live . . .'

'She talked about "Debbie's flat" not "our flat" so I assumed that they don't live together. I haven't got their addresses because I just listened to what she told me. I thought I shouldn't ask any questions until you . . .'

'You did right. Go on.'

'As far as I can make out from the little she said about what actually happened, the man who kidnapped them, there was only one at that point, was hidden in the back of their car when they got in. She doesn't know how he got through the main doors and an electronically operated gate to get in to the courtyard where the car is always left unlocked. I got the impression that the car actually belongs to the American girl but I'm not certain. The man must obviously have been armed to have kidnapped two adults single-handed but she didn't say so. I thought it best not to press her.'

'Good. It was one of the girls then that drove the car out of Florence?'

'Yes, the Maxwell girl. Somewhere past Pontino, the

last village she remembers seeing, they were told to turn into a narrow lane where they were met by a small truck. They were made to lie down on the floor in the back. The truck later delivered this girl to the place where she was dumped on the outskirts of Pontino. The injury to her knee she did herself by falling against a tree in the dark.'

'How is it?'

'They say it's deep and will leave quite a scar. Even so, it's only a flesh wound and will heal in ten days or so. I imagine it must have been a cypress tree since they prune the lower branches leaving a swordlike edge sticking up. As for her head injury, the immediate danger's past but her sight and balance have to be checked once she's able to get up, which will be today, I think.'

'They'll bring her down to Florence in that case?'

'Yes, later this morning. There's only the local GP here and twice a week a doctor from Poggibonsi does a round. Any seriously ill patients are usually sent to a state hospital.'

'I'll see her later today then. It would help if they put her in San Giovanni.'

The hospital of San Giovanni di Dio was practically next door to Headquarters, which was convenient in the case of patients who required a permanent guard or who had to be questioned at intervals.

'I'll mention it. I suppose it depends where there's a bed. Do you think it was a mistake, sir? Their taking this girl as well?'

'I don't know. But these people don't usually make mistakes.'

'They're professionals, then?'

The Substitute, too, had said, 'In that case we surely are talking about professionals . . .' And it was true that the Captain was proceeding as though they were. Even so, he only said again:

'I don't know.' Then he added, 'You ought to get some

sleep. I'll phone the Brigadier up there and tell him to send a man to relieve you.'

'I think I should stay, sir, if you agree. I promised I would and she's still very nervous, I think. Perhaps I could at least stay until she wakes up and I can explain what's happening.'

She was woken at seven by the night nurses who had to tidy her up before they went off duty. The officer waited out in the corridor and so it happened that, on leaving, one of the nurses in a hurry to get home said: 'You could take her flowers if you're going back in.'

She was propped up now against a heap of pillows. Her loose yellow hair and the white hospital nightgown made her look like a sick child. The bandage round her head had been replaced by a small dressing above one eyebrow.

'Bring them here.' She was staring at the flowers. 'Let me look at them . . .' She fingered the brightly coloured daisies as if testing whether they were real. Here and there the leaves, too, were streaked with turquoise and purple paint. 'He really was painting them.'

'That's what upset you before?' The officer was bewildered.

'Yesterday . . . Yes, I remember, I saw them when I woke up and I thought . . . It seems stupid now but you can't imagine what it was like stumbling about in the dark and then seeing him daubing away . . . whoever heard of painted flowers . . .'

'But otherwise they'd all be white,' explained the officer reasonably. 'There aren't many flowers about so early in the year. These daisies are quite plentiful.'

'But all white.'

'Yes.'

'So they paint them.'

'Yes. The florist brought them. He found you but I suppose you don't remember.'

'That was nice of him, to bring the flowers. And I

thought he was a nightmare or that I was going out of my mind. You'll have to move your hat.'

He picked it up and set the flowers down on the locker.

'Aren't you going to sit down?'

'No, I have to leave now. They'll soon be taking you down to Florence.'

'But won't you be coming with me . . .?' She stopped and blushed at the stupidity of the question, adding quickly, 'You work here in the village, of course.'

'No.' It was he who blushed now at being taken for a country bumpkin. 'I work in Florence. There's a guard from the local station here outside your door. A car will follow you down in the ambulance and they'll send a guard from Headquarters to stay with you once you get there.'

'Am I in danger?'

'Probably not but we don't take any risks.'

'But . . . If you work in Florence can't they send you?'

'Send me?'

'To the hospital where they take me—instead of people I don't know?'

The young man's face darkened even more.

'I don't do guard duty,' he said, 'I'm an officer. I was sent out here because we thought you probably spoke English. Your Italian . . .'

'I know it's not very good . . . But you will come sometime . . . I mean . . .'

'I shall probably be there to translate when the Captain in charge of the case questions you.' To his distress he saw that she was trembling slightly. He saluted briefly and opened the door, afraid that she might be about to cry. He was somewhat mollified by the fact that the Brigadier's boy, Sartini, snapped to attention as he passed, well within her view.

'What time did they find the car?'

'First thing this morning, more or less.'

The Brigadier was bouncing the jeep once again along the road out of Pontino, sending up sprays of wet grit and grumbling continually under his breath, this time because he had to keep switching the wipers on and off. A keen wind was puffing small clouds across the pale blue sky, blotting out the sun and sending miniature showers against his windscreen. A draught whistled through the jeep and all three men had the collars of their mackintoshes turned up. The Substitute also had a large English umbrella which lay in the back beside his briefcase and a brand new pair of green galoshes. By this time he and the Captain were accustomed to conversing against a background of the Brigadier's *sotto voce* lamentations.

'The lads searched that whole area yesterday—'the Captain indicated the vineyards and cornfields to their left—'And started on the other side this morning. They found the car almost immediately since it wasn't particularly well hidden.'

'How much will it help?'

'Probably not a great deal but it's a loose end tied up. It would help, of course, if someone had seen it being dumped, but I'm afraid that even if someone did—'

'Here we are,' announced the Brigadier, emerging suddenly from his world of private woes and turning right on to a grassy track running between two olive groves. Where the trees finished the track dipped sharply down through neglected fields to a narrow valley watered by a stream.

'Have to leave the jeep and walk from here on.'

They had to wait while the Substitute put on his new galoshes, murmuring with a cigar between his teeth: 'Don't want to miss anything this time . . .'

The wooden bridge over the stream had to be crossed in single file. On the other side the ground began to slope up again.

'And how did they get the car across here?' asked the

Substitute, slowing to put a flame to a freshly filled pipe. The tobacco smelt sweet on the sharp air.

'They'll have come by the villa,' said the Brigadier enigmatically.

'Ah . . .'

'We'll go back that way. I like to keep my eye on Pratesi at the sausage factory.'

The villa came into view on the brow of the hill above them. A balustrade ran round its flat roof with terra cotta urns at each corner, outlined sharply against the blue sky.

'Not that that's much of a road to speak of,' the Brigadier went on, 'But the family hasn't lived there since before the war—there were German and then English soldiers billeted here during the second war . . .'

The Substitute would have been willing to bet every cigar he had on him that the Brigadier had been about to add 'before you were born'. He had been bemused at first by the scraps of peripheral information the Brigadier periodically tossed them with the air of someone indulging an already overfed dog, but now he was beginning to understand. Out of habit the Brigadier treated everybody as though they were local National Service boys who had grown up in the village and so knew every blade of grass as well as he did but who might be a bit hazy about certain family backgrounds and about things that had happened before their time. Once he had even got as far as adding 'before you . . .' and then tailed off into his private grumbles.

'He lives in Torino,' the Brigadier offered them now.

'Who does?'

'The old Count.' He nodded at the villa. 'There's talk of him coming back.'

'And how does he get away with this?' The Captain looked about him with disgust. The vineyards on each side of their path were tangled and choked with weeds. The rioting, spent vines had grown black tentacles in all directions, sprouting now with fresh green shoots and hung with ghostly old man's beard. The undergrowth must have been a haven for vipers and the three men kept strictly to the path. According to the law, neglected land could be confiscated by the state.

'That's how.' The Brigadier stabbed the air in front of him.

At the top of the hill near the last curve of the weedy driveway that led round from the back of the villa a young man stood watching their approach.

''Morning, Rudolfo.' The Brigadier was panting a little as they reached the top of the slope.

The young man had deep-set black eyes and very high cheekbones. He smiled uncertainly, showing white teeth.

'You're down early,' remarked the Brigadier in a friendly tone.

'I'm not down, I'm still grazing the mountain but I wanted to get some planting done.'

'At this time?'

'Potatoes.'

'Good lad. Did they find the car on your patch?'

'No, in the next field, or rather in the ditch between.'

'The villa been searched?'

'No.'

'Well, it will be. Don't worry about it.'

'The gamekeeper's got the keys.'

'Is he in?'

'He's gone to the market.'

'Then he'll not be back until lunch-time. Don't worry about it,' the Brigadier repeated. 'You get on with your potatoes.'

'Who is he?' asked the Captain as they followed the Brigadier across a wet field. Black figures could be seen milling round the ditch at the far end of it.

'Giovanni Fara. He's a good lad.'

'Didn't you call him Rudolfo?'

'Seeing as everybody else does,' said the Brigadier, 'I do too.'

The other two pondered over this morsel as they tramped along behind him. Half way across the field to the ditch where a jeep was now straining at a rope attached to the emerging car, the Substitute lit on a possible solution.

'Rudolph Valentino!' he exclaimed, drawing an odd look from the Captain. 'He looks just like him!'

'And he's a good lad,' continued the Brigadier, taking this masterpiece of deduction in his stride. 'His mother's widowed back in Sardinia and there are two smaller children, a lad of fourteen who's here helping Rudolfo and a girl at home with her mother. He's struggling along at present with fifty or so sheep, growing a bit of food for himself along with his winter feed for the beasts. In a year or two he should have a decent sized flock—of course he's not normally down here this early, he only has a bit of a stable down here that he rents for the summer along with his few acres of grass and his bit of land for cultivation. His cottage is up on the mountain and he'll be grazing up there . . .'

'Until Palm Sunday,' finished the Substitute automatically.

'Anyway,' the Brigadier wound up as they stood peering into the ditch, 'that's how he gets away with it.'

'What . . .?' The Captain had lost him.

'The Count. Between Rudolfo and the gamekeeper there's just enough of the land being cultivated for it not to be confiscated. That's the only reason they're there.'

The Captain took a look at the car's registration number as his men scraped the mud and twigs away. The fingerprint expert was unpacking his bag. A television cameraman was circling the car slowly with a hand-held camera.

'What story are you giving them?' murmured the Substitute.

A group of reporters stood gossiping and smoking nearby, their shoes sunk deep into the muddy field, their faces reddened by the wind.

'There wasn't anything much I could tell them yesterday.'

'Even so, it seems they went to the American Consulate.'

'I suppose they would . . .' The Captain, having been at work since the call from the hospital at six, had not had time to read the morning paper. No doubt the Substitute read the newspapers at the same breakneck speed as he did everything else.

'They're not giving you any trouble?'

'The Consulate? No, no . . .' He didn't add that when he had first telephoned them they hadn't wanted to know. The official he had spoken to had only said:

'There's no proof that this person is an American citizen?'

'No proof, no. But as there was a telephone message to be—'

'We haven't received any message.'

'No, it was never sent.'

'And no one's reported this girl missing?'

'No. Nevertheless, perhaps you would inform the Consul General. If there are any developments that concern you I'll let you know.'

The Captain hadn't insisted. It was natural enough not to want this sort of problem to deal with if it wasn't absolutely necessary. As long as they had been promptly informed he was covered for any eventuality. The fewer people he had to cope with, the better.

'What I haven't told them,' he said, glancing again at the journalists, 'is that the released girl had a message to deliver and didn't deliver it. Before I tell them that I need to talk to the girl. Then it may be necessary to have them publish something that could help us.'

'The contents of the message?'

'Without knowing what it is I can't say—and it's not something I can rush because the girl won't talk if she's frightened, or she'll talk but not tell us the truth. It's more than likely that I'll ask them to publish that we know there's a message but that she hasn't delivered it and won't talk. The sooner we can get these people to make contact themselves, the better. Until they do I'm working completely in the dark.'

A helicopter flew low over their heads and turned in a tight circle. One of the uniformed men on the ground spoke into his radio, looking up.

'They'll go on patrolling?' asked the Substitute.

'Certainly. They know what they're looking for if not who. Smoke coming from a normally disused building, a vehicle heading for a deserted spot. In an area like this all the vehicles and their normal movements are known.'

'Of course.' The Substitute looked to where the Brigadier was deep in conversation with a group of men from the Captain's company. Two of the Brigadier's boys were working with them and one of them was giving a complicated description of some distant patch of ground with the aid of both arms. 'Every blade of grass . . .'

The fingerprint man was packing up. Another technician poked his head out of the car to ask:

'Is there anything you want to look at here?'

The Captain glanced inside. A box of tissues, some of them crumpled, gloves, a torch, a map lying on the back seat. He took a look at the map in case anything was marked on it. There was nothing.

'Take everything down to Florence with you. You can phone a preliminary report to my office tomorrow . . .' Normally he would have said 'as soon as you can'. Perhaps it was only because of the Substitute's presence that he added, 'At eleven o'clock,' and then turned away quickly because the technician was about to protest. 'We have to talk to Piladu . . .'

It meant going back to the village first and taking another road out. The market was in full swing as they made their way slowly round the piazza, the Brigadier leaning on the horn to make a path through the jumble of cars and people milling about in the bright but fitful sunshine. He looked for the gamekeeper from the villa among the group of men in dark suits and flat caps who stood talking between the plastic flower stall and the van selling salted fish, but he wasn't able to spot him. Once out of the village they picked up speed and took a road that would zigzag through five hamlets before bringing them to the only cart track that wound up the lower slopes of the mountain. The track, the Brigadier explained to them patiently, was all that was left from the days when the mountain villages were inhabited. There had been partisans hidden up there during the war, before you . . . but now only the shepherds used the long-abandoned houses and they went up on foot with their flocks. By the time they were lurching slowly along the cart track the wind had dropped, letting the clouds gather. It began to rain steadily as they stopped the jeep where the track met two barely discernible footpaths.

'Three Valleys Pass,' announced the Brigadier, switching off the engine. They could hear the rain pattering in the grass and bouncing off the roof of the jeep. There wasn't a soul in sight but the Brigadier got out and called up to his left:

'Pil-a . . . du!'

They waited a long time and nobody appeared but the Brigadier didn't call again. It was true that in such a solitary place anyone within a dozen miles must have heard him. He got back into the jeep for shelter. It was five or six minutes later that Piladu appeared on the mountainside, stared at them for sometime and then tramped slowly towards them tightly wrapped in his hooded cloak. He stopped a few yards away and waited.

'You can get in,' the Brigadier said, 'if you want to.' The rain was coming down harder in big drops. Piladu didn't move.

'We want to know what your son had to say.'

'He never came home.' There was no trace of his usual cheekiness, either because he was seriously worried about his son or simply because he had no need to defend himself up here where he was in his element and they were out of theirs. It was impossible to tell which from his expressionless gaze. He looked slightly past them as if they had already been and gone.

'When was the last time he came home?' persisted the Brigadier.

'Two nights ago.'

'Was Scano's boy with him?'

'I didn't see him.'

The rain rolled off his thick greasy cloak that had strands of wool and stiff patches of dried blood down the front. The old dog ambled lamely towards them, shook his wet pelt and stood shivering beside his master. They could hear the younger dog in the distance, his bark muffled now by the rapidly descending cloud.

'And you say he's not on drugs?'

'I say he's no business hanging around Florence. His place is here with me.' It was plain enough now, from the glance he shot in the general direction of the three of them and the jeep, that so far as he was concerned they were just part and parcel of the trouble generated by the city, the days he had to spend queuing in the tax office, the months he had spent shut up in the squalid, overcrowded prison, the endless haggling with shopkeepers, the disappearance of his good-for-nothing son.

When they eventually let him go, he paused and spat

deliberately, sideways into the grass. The dog, his head low against the rain, walked stiffly at his heels. They watched until the cloud hid him from view.

'What about the rest of it?' asked the Substitute, lighting a cigarette, 'Up there. Mightn't the girl be hidden on the mountain?' He was craning his neck to look up but nothing was visible except the rolling grey mist that had almost reached the jeep.

'I'm quite sure,' said the Captain slowly, 'that she is.'

'You want a warrant?'

'No. I don't want a warrant. I want to know who's got her and I want to know exactly where. Otherwise we could search up there for a year and we wouldn't find her.'

'It's not worth trying a surprise raid?'

'You can't surprise a mountain. There are no roads up there and not a square metre of flat ground where a helicopter could land. They'd see us coming hours before we got up there on foot, the girl would have been spirited away before we got anywhere near her and nobody would speak to us except in their incomprehensible dialect. For the most part they wouldn't speak at all even if threatened. They're not like Piladu who lives in the valley.'

The Substitute, who had not considered Piladu very communicative up to then, fell to smoking in silence. The Brigadier switched on the motor and they began a bumpy, swaying descent. Thunder was grumbling somewhere in the distance. As the jeep turned the last curve at the foot of the slope the Brigadier braked and pointed.

'See those rocks.' They were scattered everywhere, great lumps of the white flint of which the mountain was formed. As they looked, one of the rocks in the distance moved to one side and stopped, then moved again. 'Sheep,' said the Brigadier. 'And it could just as easily be the shepherd lying still with an old sheepskin thrown over him. An old trick but it still works. You wouldn't notice him unless you fell over him. You can't surprise a mountain.' He was pleased with this phrase of the Captain's and was evidently storing it up for his National Service boys. He loosed the brakes and the jeep rolled onwards.

Their ten-kilometre drive out to Scano's place was a waste of time. There was no sign of the son, an undersized, sly creature who had spent more time in prison than out of it ever since he had been old enough to get himself down to the city and into trouble. He normally hung about the house all day and disappeared before his father brought the sheep back from pasture so as to avoid milking time. They knocked for a good ten minutes before giving up but it was obvious that the place was deserted. The rain beat against the peeling door and the uncurtained windows and dripped from the still bloody lambskin that swung spreadeagled from the washing line.

'Let's get back to Florence.' The Captain swung himself into the jeep. He was wet, cold and irritable and he was already losing patience with this case. What sort of kidnapping was this, with no ransom demand and no parents? And to cap it all, it had to be on a case as weird as this that they sent him a Substitute Prosecutor who watched his performance with amused detachment. He felt like a circus. The whole thing was irregular.

After dropping off the Substitute, the Captain went to his office before going to lunch. He wasn't expecting much to have come in during his absence but if nothing else there should be something from the foreign residents department at the Questura. The note was on his desk. The missing girl, Deborah Jean Maxwell, was an American citizen. Occupation: student. Resident in Piazza Pitti, No. 3. The Captain sat down and reached for the telephone. His face had relaxed. If he ever found this girl he would thank her for choosing to live in that quarter of the city. After a surfeit of the extraordinary this was just what he needed: a dose of the solidly ordinary.

'Yessir!'

'Get me Marshal Guarnaccia at Pitti.'

CHAPTER 6

The Marshal was out. He had taken the van that morning from the gravelled patch outside his Station in the left wing of the Pitti Palace and driven across the city to the Appeal Court in Via Cavour. It was a case that bothered him because he felt that in the Assize Court the unfortunate man's chances had been wrecked by that fool of a cocky young barrister who had concocted an elaborate defence that gave a totally false impression of what had happened. By grossly exaggerating the victim's treatment of the accused in order to gain sympathy for the latter he had instead made it seem all the more likely that he had meant to kill. The only time little Cipolla had been allowed to speak was when they had asked him:

'Did you intend to fire the gun when you picked it up?'

'Yes . . . but . . .'

'Just answer the question.'

Without that damned barrister there could well have been a verdict of accidental death.

The Marshal had arrived in time, as he had promised, to see Cipolla delivered to the court and taken upstairs, chained between two other prisoners whose appeals were to be heard that morning. During the fifteen months that he had been in prison his black hair had turned grey and his features had lost their definition. The Marshal always used to think he looked childlike, being so small, but now he was a little old man. Nevertheless, he had cast the Marshal a grateful look when he saw him standing there as promised, watching with his big, slightly bulging eyes.

It was a long dull wait. After a while the Marshal climbed the stairs in the hope of getting an idea of what was going on. He could hear only a faint murmur of voices from behind the closed door. The guard outside was chainsmoking. The cracked brown linoleum under his feet was littered with cigarette ends. The Marshal nodded to him and started back down the ill-lit, dusty staircase. Half way down he heard a commotion below and quickened his heavy step in time to see, as he turned the last bend in the staircase, a slight figure slip out through the iron gate at the main entrance. When the Marshal opened the gate and looked out into the courtyard the figure had vanished. The black van was parked under a palm tree waiting to take the prisoners back to the *Murate*. There were a dozen or so cars parked near the entrance, including the Marshal's small van, but not a soul in sight. A woman came out behind him and looked from left to right.

'You didn't catch him?'

'No.'

'That wretched man! And it's not the first time by any means.'

'What happened?'

'He steals things. It really is too much!'

'But . . . aren't you from the Ex-prisoners' Assistance? What I mean is, don't you give the stuff away, anyway?'

'We do, but there's never enough good clothing to go round so we have to keep a check on who's had what. That wretched man steals anything that's of good quality that he can get his hands on—not for himself since they're usually things that don't fit him—he sells them to the second-hand clothes stalls on San Lorenzo market.'

'I see.' They walked back inside. 'What's his name?'

I'd have to look up his real name; everybody calls him "Baffetti" because of his moustache which in my opinion makes him look just as shifty as he is. I'll look it up.'

'But really, I'm not here for—'

'A stop has to be put to it, once and for all. To crown everything, not only were we already packing up when he arrived but today's not men, it's women. He had the cheek to say he needed things for his wife who has to go into hospital.'

The room just along the corridor from where the Marshal had been waiting was stuffy and fetid with the smell of old unwashed clothing and mothballs. A few pairs of battered shoes were lined up along an old wooden shelf. A second woman was folding worn sweaters and putting them away in a scratched wardrobe. There were cardboard boxes stuffed full of clothes standing everywhere on the dusty floor.

'Here . . .' The first woman pulled out a small card from a file on the desk, 'Garau he's called, Pasqualino Garau.'

'He's been inside?'

'Yes, he has. He's perfectly entitled to come here but not to run off with anything he fancies and sell it. It's not fair to the others—and asking for clothes for his wife is about the last straw!'

'His wife should come herself on women's day? But if she really is ill . . .'

'He hasn't got a wife!'

'I see.'

'It's so unfair on other ex-prisoners who genuinely need help and who need to be decently dressed in order to try and get a job.'

The Marshal, his big eyes rolling round the depressing room lit by one dusty light-bulb because the small, barred window hardly let in any light, wondered if they ever managed it. There was such an air of hopelessness about the place.

The woman was slotting the card back into the file.

'One of you really ought to sort him out. We can't

cope—and he's not the only one.'

'I'm afraid I'm not . . . I'm here for a case that's being heard in the Appeal Court . . .'

'That poor little man, what's he called? The one who's supposed to have shot that Englishman? He doesn't look capable of harming a fly; I saw him being brought in. In any case there's a good Marshal who's . . . Oh . . .' The harassed woman looked up from her work. 'You must be . . .'

But the Marshal, with a hurried 'Good Morning,' was gone.

He heard the door open upstairs, then the sound of voices mingled with a scraping of chairs. Then a pause. The Marshal knew that the guard would be putting handcuffs and chains back on the prisoners and lighting cigarettes for them which they would smoke with both hands. Cipolla didn't smoke. There were heavy steps on the stairs. Cipolla was once again chained between the two larger men. His eyes immediately sought the Marshal's and he said, as he always said: 'Thank you, Marshal.'

Thank you for being there, for at this stage the Marshal was powerless to help him. There had been no acquittal since they were taking him back to the prison. The barrister came down along with two others, their silk gowns rustling, their noses lifted a little against the dusty air. The Marshal planted himself where he filled the exit and asked without preliminaries: 'Cipolla?'

'Sentence reduced to fifteen years. Intent to wound, no intent to kill.'

'Thank you.' He let them go by. Fifteen years. He felt sure that Cipolla wouldn't survive them. He wouldn't come out of prison alive. If he'd had the money to choose a more experienced barrister, if the Marshal himself had been on the spot in the first place instead of that young fool student, Bacci, who fancied himself as some sort of Hollywood detective, probably have shot himself accidentally by this time . . . whole thing had been a mess from start to finish . . . fifteen years . . . would have been ten if it hadn't been a gun . . . poor creature . . .

He backed his van up and drove out of the courtyard to join the heavy lunch-time traffic moving towards the Cathedral. There were clear blue gaps in the cloud here and there but light rain continued to spatter the windscreen. The usual long line of buses stopping and starting blocked the road all the way from Piazza San Marco to the Cathedral. Each time he tried to overtake, one of them would signal and pull out. Patience . . . his lunch would be cold, though . . . fifteen years.

His lunch was cold. He wasn't all that sorry to find an urgent message from Headquarters that meant leaving the glutinous pasta. He could snatch a coffee and sandwich in the bar over there at some point.

The Captain wasn't in his office. The adjutant directed him to the hospital next door, giving him written instructions on how to find the ward. The Marshal slipped them into his top pocket. He knew the hospital well enough to find the side ward without difficulty. He couldn't see the patient when he first entered because of the people standing around her. One of them, doubtless the Substitute Prosecutor, was on his feet, playing with an unlit pipe. The Captain was seated with his back to the door. The third man was the one who held the Marshal's attention. It was that young fool of a student Bacci, who stood up stiffly at the sight of the Marshal who had witnessed his first embarrassingly unsuccessful attempt at being a policeman. The Marshal stared expressionlessly at the blushing face and then at the star on the young man's epaulette. With the briefest salute at what was now his superior officer he said gravely, 'Lieutenant . . .' and turned his attention to the Captain who greeted him briefly and then continued his interrogation with the younger officer interpreting.

'You didn't see his face?'

'No.'

'Why not?'

'It was covered.'

'With what?'

'I don't know. Something black . . . perhaps it was a skiing mask.'

'You saw his eyes?'

'No. I don't know. He made us turn away. We were both in front, so . . .'

'Who drove?'

'Debbie did. He held a gun at my neck.'

'You didn't say before that he was armed.'

'He couldn't have made us do what he wanted otherwise since he was on his own.'

'He held a gun at your neck driving through the busy streets at rush hour?'

'It was hidden behind a map which he held open right behind our heads.'

The Marshal, whose thoughts were still with the prisoner on his way back to serve fifteen years in the *Murate*, and who was further distracted by half the talk being in English, was hardly able to follow a word of this interrogation. He had no idea what it was all about, anyway.

The Captain was saying to the Sub-lieutenant, 'I want to know everything she can tell us about the Maxwell girl, family, friends, habits, etcetera—everything. You needn't translate, I can follow you.'

Sub-lieutenant Bacci, very much aware of the Marshal's enormous eyes fixed upon him, began his questioning rather hesitantly. Nevertheless the girl answered him more readily than she had the Captain, her gaze fixed on his face.

'She has a father and a stepmother.'

'Does she get on with them?'

'She talks a lot about her father. I think she's very attached to him.'

'And the stepmother?'

'I don't know. She's never said anything against her. I got the impression that they didn't know each other all that well, that the marriage was fairly recent.'

'Do they live in this country?'

'No, in the States.'

'Do they have property here? A holiday villa, for instance?'

'No. They've only been here once, just after Christmas.'

'What about Christmas? They didn't spend it together?'

'She went to them, for about a week, I think. I left before her to spend Christmas at home in Norway.'

'How long did her parents stay here?'

'About two weeks in all, but not always in Florence. They spent some time in the north.'

'Did he have business there?'

'No, none. Debbie was upset that they didn't spend all their time here with her.'

'What did they do in Florence?'

'Mostly sightseeing. And some shopping, he bought his wife quite a lot of jewellery.'

'And his daughter?'

'He bought her a fur coat, as a late Christmas present.'

'Was she wearing it the day you were kidnapped?'

'No. It's still in the flat.'

'Wasn't it snowing that morning?'

'Yes, but it wasn't a bit cold.'

'Did her parents stay in the flat with her?'

'No, there's only one bedroom. They stayed at the Excelsior.'

'Did Maxwell give his daughter an allowance? Is that what she lived on?'

'Yes. A telegraphic order arrived every month.'

'Do you have any idea how much it was for?'

'Yes. She sometimes signed it over to me if she needed it urgently and hadn't time to queue at the post office. It was always for two million lire.'

'That's a lot of money for a student.'

'They could afford it, I suppose.'

The Captain interrupted: 'Do you also live on an allowance?'

'Yes, but it's about half what Debbie gets and it's paid not by my father but by his firm of ship's engineers of which he's a director. I can study anywhere I like in Europe for two years.'

'Do you wish us to inform your father about what's happened?'

'Do you have to? If it's not necessary from your point of view I'd rather you didn't. I'm of age, after all, and it would give him a terrible fright. He's had one minor heart attack already, I wouldn't like to cause him another.'

'Then we'll leave it to you. Lieutenant . . . Something about their contacts and daily habits . . .'

But the girl had understood.

'We study Italian for four hours every weekday morning at the Cultural Centre for Foreigners. After that we would go back to my flat which I share with two other students in the Santa Croce area, or to Debbie's. She didn't much like to be on her own.'

'But she didn't invite you to share her flat?'

'I suppose she wasn't used to sharing since she's an only child. Most of us only share for financial reasons. She didn't have to.'

'What did you do with the rest of the day?'

'We always had homework to do. Later on we would walk round town and maybe go to the cinema. Occasionally Debbie would buy a dress.'

'Is that how she spent her allowance? On clothes?'

'Only very occasionally, when the mood took her.'

'Did she spend much on restaurants, on living well in general, on entertaining?'

'No, very little.'

'In that case what did she do with all her money? It must have accumulated. And she didn't have a bank account?'

'No. That's why she would sometimes sign the order over to me so that I could put it through my account—otherwise she had to queue up at the post office, as I said.'

'You paid her in cash?'

'Yes.'

'So where did she keep the rest of the money?'

'I don't know. I suppose it must be somewhere in the flat . . .'

The Captain signed to him to change the subject.

'Why did she come to Italy?'

'She said she wanted the experience.'

'Did she have any boyfriends?'

The girl hesitated and then said: 'One or two . . .'

'Nobody special?'

'No.'

Again the Captain made a sign and began dictating questions for translation.

Did they go to any one bar or meeting place regularly?

Did she take her father to any such place when he was here?

Did she talk about her family circumstances at school, out of school, in bars or restaurants, to her boyfriend?

Did the father know other people here independently of his daughter?

All negatives. And yet somebody had known she was worth kidnapping, somebody had checked on her financial position and her daily movements, probably over a long period.

The girl was growing pale. Two red spots high on her

cheekbones suggested that there was still a trace of fever. She had also become very tense. The Captain was aware that at this stage she was still sufficiently frightened by what had happened to her to be hiding something, but experience told him that it would be useless to try and force her. It was a situation that required patience and a certain amount of cunning.

'We'll leave you to get some rest,' he said gently, in slow, clear Italian. 'And as soon as you feel well enough I want you to write a list of everybody that the Signorina Maxwell knows in Florence. Everybody, including shopkeepers, bar owners and all the members of your class at the University—they don't have to have been special friends, just acquaintances—teachers, too. Write them down. Do you understand?' She nodded. 'Sub-lieutenant Bacci here will stay and help you in case you leave any gaps.'

The three others rose to leave and it was only at the very last moment that he added, almost casually: 'What message were you supposed to phone to the American Consulate?'

She hesitated, looking from one to the other of their expectant faces, and there was quite a distinct change in her voice as she repeated in Italian:

'Mr Maxwell, we have Deborah. The price is one and a half milliardi.'

'They gave it to you in Italian?'

'Yes. I had to repeat it a number of times so that there could be no misunderstanding. I was to speak to the Consul General.'

'You won't need that token now.'

The outline of her clenched fist was visible under the white counterpane. She looked down at it as though it belonged to somebody else, then drew it slowly out. The young officer took the token from her sweating palm. For the first time since properly regaining consciousness she asked: 'What will happen to her if nobody knows, if nobody pays, what will they do to . . .?' Her face had slackened and she was crying but without any sound.

'Let us worry about that,' said the Captain, who knew exactly what would happen if nobody paid and that they would in all likelihood never find the body. 'You have a rest and then make that list which will help us to find her. I've already telephoned the Consulate,' he added, in the hope of soothing her with a half-truth.

'What do you think?' the Captain asked Marshal Guarnaccia once they were outside and walking the two or three yards back to Headquarters.

'I didn't understand more than three words,' said the Marshal placidly. 'And she's lying.'

Beside him, the Substitute burst into delighted laughter and said, 'Maestrangelo, introduce me to this man!'

'I beg your pardon. Substitute Prosecutor Fusarri, Virgilio; Marshal Guarnaccia, Salvatore.'

They shook hands outside the sentry room, where the Substitute had a taxi called and got into it still smiling at the Marshal's deadly serious remark. 'You'll need a warrant,' was his parting observation, 'to search that flat. I'll send it over immediately. Let me know what you find.'

'New man?' asked the Marshal, staring after the taxi with bulging expressionless eyes.

'Yes.'

'Funny. He looks . . .'

'As if he only happens to be with us by accident and could just easily be amusing himself at some other job elsewhere.'

'Something like that. I wouldn't know how to put it into words.'

'We'd better go up to my office.' They went along the old cloister and up the stone stairs.

'An interesting man, the Substitute,' said the Captain as they settled into deep leather chairs, 'and intelligent.

But he's eccentric. I shall be glad to have you working with me for a while.'

The Marshal raised questioning eyebrows.

'The girl who's missing—you'll have had my circular—is Deborah Jean Maxwell and she lives in Piazza Pitti, number three.'

'I see.'

'I need to know all about her.'

'I don't know the name.'

'We'll get you a photograph.'

'I'll see what I can do. When did it happen?'

'Just after eight in the morning on the first of March.'

The Marshal frowned. After a moment he said: 'That was the day it was snowing.'

'It was. That should help since a lot of people will remember that morning because of the snow.'

'I'm not so sure . . .'

'You'd better come to the flat with me for a start, as soon as the warrant arrives. I want to take a handful of good men and go over it with a fine-tooth comb. We should be able to find a photograph for you—are you all right? You don't look your usual self.'

'I've just come from the Appeal Court. Cipolla.'

'He didn't get off?'

'Fifteen years. They quashed the murder charge but he got ten years for intent to wound resulting in death, plus, of course, half as much again because there was a firearm involved.'

'It was the only alterative to an acquittal, you knew that.'

He won't last because there's nobody waiting for him and you know what conditions are like in there. He'll catch some illness or other, I can see it coming.'

'You did your best. After all's said and done, he did shoot the man.'

'If I'd known what was going on in that house right under my nose . . .'

'You can't be everywhere at once, and you were desperately short staffed.'

'Bacci . . .' At last the Marshal smiled. 'How is he getting on?'

'Well.'

'He was lucky to get a posting here at home.'

'He's the only son of a widow and there's a young sister to support.'

'Of course. I'd forgotten.'

'Now then, there are two areas I want you to investigate as unobtrusively as possible. First, see what you can dig up about this girl's daily life in general. I want to know what sort of people she frequents outside school. I can send you a plainclothes man if necessary, somebody young who can pretend to be looking for her.'

'And second?'

'I want to know exactly what happened that morning. I want to know how this man got into the courtyard—somebody must have opened the main door and gate for him and it's possible that somebody going out may have seen him. He can hardly have been wearing a ski mask in the street at that hour of the morning, whether it was snowing or not.'

'I'll inquire,' the Marshal said.

While they were waiting for the warrant to arrive the Captain telephoned the American Consulate to inform them of Deborah Maxwell's citizenship. He spoke to a different person this time, younger and more sympathetic.

'We may be some time finding Mr Maxwell but we'll let you know as soon as we do.'

'You know him, then?'

The young man seemed embarrassed, as if he had said too much, though he had barely said anything. 'I don't know him personally,' he said, deliberately misinterpreting the question, 'but we'll do all we can and be in touch with you.'

The Captain put the receiver down thoughtfully, accepting a sheet of paper from the Adjutant who had just tapped and walked in.

'Funny . . .' he said and glanced absently at the paper.

PROCURA DELLA REPUBBLICA—Florence.
Prot/6460/80
Further to the investigation of the kidnapping of
MAXWELL Deborah Jean the Public Prosecutor
orders that the Officers of the Polizia Giudiziaria . . .

The Captain looked at his watch. 'I wouldn't have believed it,' he murmured, 'if I hadn't seen it. Perhaps he had it already made out . . .'

The Marshal only stared at the warrant, his great eyes bulging more than ever.

'Not the usual kind of student's flat,' muttered the Marshal, surprised to find his feet walking on fitted carpet, a thing that only happened to him in the lobbies of hotels he was checking on.

'Not the usual sort of student,' the Captain said, remembering that the Marshal had followed little of the bilingual conversation in the hospital, 'given that she had two million a month to spend.'

The Marshal frowned. It was the Captain who voiced his opinion for him: 'It's no wonder we can't find flats for our boys when they want to get married, with this sort of competition. Seven hundred thousand a month . . .' He had a copy of the contract in his hand.

'Still, it wasn't exactly that I was thinking of,' the Marshal said. 'I was thinking that whenever I've been into a student's flat there was a different atmosphere . . . a lot of things pinned up on the walls, for instance posters mostly . . .'

'The explanation's here.' The Captain flicked at the contract. 'Nothing shall be affixed to the walls by any method or the paintings removed from their present places . . .'

The paintings were evidently of no great value, but such as they were, they were genuine: a seventeenth-century Venus in oils in the drawing-room, some eighteenth-century engravings along the carpeted passage which led from the front door past the day rooms to the bedroom at the end. A dull portrait in oils hung in the dining-room which opened on to the drawing-room.

Small glass chandeliers tinkled in every room as the Captain's men worked their way rapidly through the apartment, leaving no trace of their visit behind them. The furniture was all good antique and some of the drawers were difficult to open and shut.

'Even so,' mused the Captain, 'you're right. Apart from there being nothing on the walls, there's very little of the personal here considering that she's lived here six months. Perhaps that little television there is hers. It looks new and it isn't listed on the inventory.' It was in bright red plastic in contrast to the muted greens and browns of everything else. It stood on a little round table in front of the muslin-curtained window, and the long green plush sofa against the opposite wall bore the imprint of the length of the girl's body as though she habitually lay there to watch it. There were a few books on a revolving mahogany stand, mostly museum catalogues. An address book lay by the telephone on a writing-desk by the door. It contained almost exclusively American names and addresses. The Captain slipped it into his pocket.

The Marshal had wandered through into the dining-room where lined foolscap and a box of pens and pencils lying between a pair of silver candlesticks suggested that the oak table was used for homework rather than for dining. They had seen a tiny marble-topped table in the kitchen, big enough for one person to eat at, perhaps two at a squash. There had been the mouldering remains of a delicatessen meal in tinfoil trays in the fridge, along with a bottle of beer and two of orange squash.

When the men had finished searching the bedroom the Captain and the Marshal went in. The same dull green carpet, two beds with carved green satin headboards, the light from the busy street filtered by a thick white muslin curtain. Despite the noise of the traffic out in the piazza, the room had a peaceful sense of intimacy about it which may have had something to do with the large low beds and the subtle green and white colours. The Captain opened a few drawers in the dressing-table. The bottom one contained bedlinen and towels, the next sweaters and blouses, the top one underwear. In one of the two miniature drawers that flanked the mirror he found a letter from the girl's father, postmarked New York. The Norwegian girl had said their home was in Michigan. He slipped the letter into his pocket. The other little drawer contained a jumble of trinkets and keepsakes; some, like the pearl drop on a gold chain, were valuable; others, like a battered old Mickey Mouse pencil-sharpener, must have had sentimental value.

The green, flower-painted wardrobe opened squeakily. The fur coat was hanging under a cotton cover. There were only a few dresses but these were elaborate, expensive and curiously old-fashioned compared to the heap of jeans and dungarees piled up on the floor of the wardrobe. The Captain ran a finger lightly down a black silk sleeve. 'I wonder where she goes in these . . .'

The Marshal was examining a photograph that was propped on a fifteenth-century prayer stool by the bed. It showed a large, plump man, already balding but with a pink, childlike face. A girl stood next to him with her arm round him. She had long brown hair and she too was fairly heavily built; she had the same childlike face, which on her was pretty.

'You'd better keep it,' the Captain said, looking over his shoulder.

They both glanced into the bathroom. An old-fashioned, green-painted bath on claw feet, a lot of bottles on the glass shelf in front of a gilded, slightly spotted mirror, everything tidy apart from a wad of used cotton wool on the edge of the sink.

'Captain?'

'You've finished? The money . . .?'

'Nothing. Just over a hundred thousand in notes of ten in the drawer next to the telephone, some change on the fridge in the kitchen. The money's not here.'

'Then she spent it and I'd like to know what on. The porter's wife who let us in might be worth talking to. It's more than possible that she cleans up here . . .'

'We have to finish tidying up in the kitchen, sir.'

'Carry on. The Marshal and I will be down in the porter's lodge.'

The porter's lodge was an over-furnished, windowless space as depressing as the porter's wife. The Captain had no sooner opened his mouth to say: 'Your husband isn't in . . .?' than she took out a crumpled handkerchief and huge tears were rolling down her fat cheeks.

'Don't name that man to me, don't mention him!'

'We only want to know—'

'He's the one who's porter here, not me. He's the one who gets the wages for it while I haven't a lira to myself not even to buy a pair of stockings, stuck here in this gloomy hole day after day—and he goes out working, he goes out to work when according to the contract he's not allowed, I should be allowed but not him. I want a divorce, that's what I want, but he'll not budge as long as he's drawing two salaries and has me cooking for him—but I'll not eat with him, I stick myself in that tiny kitchen in there—can you imagine the life I lead? But my solicitor says don't budge because if I lose this place where can I go? He's evil, that's what he is and nobody knows what I suffer. If it comes to court you two can testify. I was the one who let you in. I was the one who was here and not a sign of *him*—you can speak for me—'

'Marshal . . .' The Captain was backing away.

'All right.'

'I'll go up and see if they're ready to lock up . . .'

The Marshal sat down in the gloom at the plush-covered table and faced the tearful woman across a bowl of plastic fruit. Her rolled-up handkerchief was already soaked through but she went on twisting it round and round in her fingers and dabbing at her wet face.

The Captain's men were already clattering down the broad stone staircase, ignoring the slow old lift. He turned to join them and then heard the telephone ringing inside the flat. The door was still open until the weeping woman should come up and lock it. He ran along the carpeted passage and into the drawing-room where he picked up the phone without speaking. After a moment a man's voice said in Italian:

'Is it you?'

There was no point in not answering so he said:

'Do you want to speak to Miss Maxwell?'

The caller hung up.

CHAPTER 7

'What sort of time would it have been?'

'Between eight and eight-thirty.'

'At that time I'm usually taking the children to school.'

'I know,' said the Marshal patiently, 'that's why I thought you might have seen something.'

The woman pondered, pushing the baby's pram to and fro absently.

'It's so long ago . . .'

'Almost three weeks ago.'

'If you'd asked me nearer the time . . .'

'You weren't here. We've already checked everyone in the piazza once.'

For all the good it had done. It was the same story every time: nothing at all until at last the significance of the date went home— 'But that was the day it was snowing, don't you remember?' 'Yes, I remember.' 'It was in the paper. They say the world's shifting on its axis, there could be another ice age.' 'But did you notice . . .?'

It was never any good. They had only noticed the snow. Now it was Signora Rosi's turn.

'Wait a minute! You said the first of March? But that was the day it was snowing, I remember now!'

There was no point in getting angry. After all, what did the Marshal himself remember about that morning other than the snow? Time and again he had rolled the scene through his memory. It was a knack he had. If anyone asked him what had happened on a certain occasion he wasn't able to tell them right off because he never put his memories into words. Yet, given time, he could roll back any given scene like a film and look at it again, stopping and starting the images at will, examining areas and details that he hadn't noticed at the time. It was a slow process, of course. He had a reputation for being a bit slow-witted but it didn't perturb him in the least. He was accustomed to it from his schooldays since his wasn't a memory system that made a good impression on harassed teachers or impatient examiners, especially as it didn't work at all with books.

He let Signora Rosi go on her way, wheeling the baby through the courtyard of the Pitti Palace into the Boboli Gardens to take the afternoon air along with the other mothers and babies of the Quarter.

The sharp bright sunshine, accompanied by cold winds and interspersed with long periods of heavy rain, had at last given way to real spring weather, warm sunshine and feathery showers. The Marshal crossed the sunny fore-court towards the shadow of the stone archway and into his office, where he could take off the dark glasses which he always had to wear when the sun was out. He sat down heavily at his desk and sighed. The first warm weather always had this same effect on him, a feeling of elation followed by a bad bout of homesickness. At home in Syracuse it would be quite hot by now, the almond blossoms and the big purple thistles blooming. Hot enough to sit out in the Piazza studded with big brown and green palms against the rose-coloured stucco of the buildings and perhaps try a first ricotta ice-cream. He gazed dully out of the little window at a dark, neatly-clipped laurel hedge and the gravel path where the black cars were parked. What was he supposed to be thinking about? That morning in the snow . . .

Slowly he ran through the scene, saw the big flakes falling, the boy in the white apron scattering sawdust, the cars coming towards him. He stopped, remembering. A car was coming towards him, signalling. Someone in the back was holding a map. He had been through it before and had already told the Captain he was sure that was the car, though he hadn't looked at the driver and front passenger, having been distracted by the map and by watching the traffic coming from all three directions because he wanted to cross over. It wasn't all that much help, anyway, as far as tracing the kidnappers was concerned, but it did mean that on that point at least the Nilsen girl was telling the truth.

It was something else that was bothering him, something illogical that he couldn't explain to the Captain until he had explained it to himself.

Again he saw the car signalling, signalling to turn right into Via Mazzetta which was the route south out of the city. Then he was crossing the road and the long ochre-coloured palace came into view with the snowflakes falling slowly in front of it to land on the roofs of the cars parked on the sloping car park in front. A Sardinian piper was coming towards him. Just one. No matter how he looked at it, it didn't make sense. It was true that there were usually two of them together and he remembered thinking at the time that the other one was probably in a shop begging. Even so, it was all wrong. He tried again. The piper was coming towards him wrapped in a black cloak, playing . . . what had he been playing? The Marshal couldn't for the life of him remember that. Normally you didn't think about it. At Christmas they always played 'You came down from the stars' and at Easter they usually played a Pastorale, and what with the roar of the traffic and the crowds of chattering shoppers or tourists it was practically impossible to distinguish the tune except in short bursts. Everybody just assumed that that's what they were playing. Nobody took much notice. Some Florentines liked them because they were picturesque. They would give them money and accept the little religious pictures or good luck messages that the shepherds handed out. Others hated and ignored them, saying they only came down to the city to steal. Certainly nobody had been taking any notice of this one—but then, hadn't he been playing very badly, anyway? And what would he have been playing? It had been neither Christmas nor Easter. The Marshal could recall no hard and fast rule about it but he couldn't think that he had ever seen the pipers during Lent. It always seemed that they reappeared around Palm Sunday when people were pouring out of the churches carrying little sprays of olive leaves that looked silvery in the hard sunlight.

The piper that morning had only worn an ordinary

shepherd's cloak, not the short swinging cape, long white woollen socks criss-crossed by leather straps . . . Well, not all of them had those things . . .

This wasn't helping at all. If the piper was early, he was early. But if he had nothing to do with the kidnapping of that girl it seemed to be too much of a coincidence that he should have appeared just then. Nobody he had questioned had seen a second piper. But then, only three people in the whole piazza remembered seeing the first one! That was the snow again . . . Odd that the Captain had thought it would help. It had done nothing but distract everybody. The kidnappers couldn't have chosen a better day.

The Marshal would have liked to turn this problem over to the Captain who could have applied some brains to it. The only thing that stopped him was that he couldn't decide exactly what the problem was. Either that Sardinian's being there was coincidence or it wasn't—and, for goodness' sake, if it wasn't—

'Marshal?' His young Brigadier, Lorenzini, clattered down the stairs and put his head round the door. 'It's half past two.'

'Yes.' The Marshal looked at him unseeingly.

'That road accident. The doctor said the driver should have come round from the anaesthetic by now.'

'Yes . . .'

Lorenzini waited and then asked: 'So do you want me to go and take his statement?'

'Yes—no. Send Di Nuccio. I'd rather you stayed here in case I have to go out.

'All right. Oh—Cipolla's sister came round when you were out before.'

The imprisoned man's sister was married to a gardener in the Boboli and lived just next door.

'She said if you could spare an hour . . . she'd just come back and said he was very low and asking for you. I did explain to her that you were on this case—'

'That's all right. I'll manage to get round there . . .'

'She left something in the kitchen for you, I think.'

She always did. Some soup or little homemade cakes, convinced that as a grass widower he couldn't cope. His wife down in Syracuse was of the same opinion. In fact, he managed perfectly well if you didn't count a certain lack of variety in his evening meals and the fact that he was forever missing the lunch that the boys brought over from the mensa dead on twelve-thirty.

'Should he take the van?'

'Who?'

'Di Nuccio. To the hospital?'

'Yes.' Now he'd lost track of what he'd been thinking of completely. And besides, there were two things bothering him at the same time and he had assumed that the second problem nagging at him had been Cipolla. But now that Lorenzini had mentioned him he realized that it wasn't. It was something more closely connected with the piper . . .

He leafed through the stack of notes that was the result of their questioning everyone in the area about what they had seen that morning. Almost every interview ended with 'I don't remember much except that it was snowing . . .' or words to that effect. Almost every interview—but there was somebody he wanted to go back and see. That was it. It stuck in his mind because she was the one person who, of course, hadn't mentioned the snow, hadn't even noticed it because of being stuck in 'that gloomy hole' as she put it herself, day in, day out, and that evil husband of hers never there, *never*! But he slept there, didn't he? The Marshal had called back a number of times and each time the woman's sobs had had a note of triumph in them.

'You see? I'm alone all the time. I'm the one who's always here to let you in, you can testify.'

But she hadn't let the kidnapper in, she could swear to that because, having pressed the switch, she always put her head out to see who was coming in since there wasn't a housephone. The first person she had opened up for that morning had been the postman at five past eight. It always was. And he had put the post in her hand personally as he always did. The Marshal had made a point of checking on that because although the Florentines spent a small fortune on electronic locks, bars, security doors and burglar alarms they quite often pressed the switches and opened up the lot to anybody with the wit to ring the bell and call '*Telegramme*!' The thief, having got past ninety per cent of the gates and gadgets blocking his way, would break into one of the flats in the building. Not the one whose bell he had rung, of course.

The Marshal stood up. If that wretched woman's husband wasn't there today, he would search the city until he found him, however slight the hope that he might know something. The woman was more concerned with gathering evidence for her divorce than with the truth, and she was determined to browbeat everyone into believing her. He buttoned up his black jacket and slid a hand into the top pocket for his sunglasses, calling up the stairs to where Lorenzini's typewriter was clacking rapidly:

'I'm going out!'

No. 3 was directly opposite the palace, only a minute away, but he was stopped twice by tourists whose thick German accents he couldn't begin to understand, and then by having to settle a violent argument between two drivers who had managed to crash while manoeuvering their cars out of their parking spaces. He eventually gave this one up and left them both threatening the car park attendant, but it took him half an hour to cross the street and ring the bell at No. 3.

Just as she had said, the porter's wife opened up the main door and the inner gate from her room and then poked her head out. Her door was set back so that she didn't see him until the was past the cars in the centre of the courtyard. He gave her no time to start crying.

'I want to speak to your husband. And if he's out—' she was reaching for the handkerchief in her apron pocket—'I want to know where he is. If he really has got another job, as you say, I want to know where.'

'Do you think he'd tell me? He hasn't spoken to me except in anger for nine years!'

'Then how are you going to prove in court that he's breaking his contract here by working somewhere else?'

'I know he works in a restaurant. I know that. But only from my neighbours, not from him.'

'Which neighbours?'

'The porter's wife at number five.'

'You go round there talking to her?'

'How can I? You know I'm stuck here all day.'

The Marshal had seen them as they stood gossiping in the street at an equal distance between the two buildings, so as to keep their doors in view, but it would be a waste of time trying to get her to admit it.

'So she comes round here for a gossip?'

'She comes to see me.'

'How often?'

'Quite often. When she can.'

'Every day?'

'Usually when she goes shopping . . .'

'Every morning, that is.'

'If I had a husband like hers—even so, underneath they're all as bad. If I had my time over again—'

'How does she know where your husband works?'

'Because she's seen him with her own eyes! And she'll testify—she's as good as said so, unlike some who don't—'

'If she's seen him with her own eyes she knows which restaurant it is.' Blood out of a stone! The Marshal was red in the face. They should have known all along that she was lying but everyone was in a hurry to get away from her embarrassing tears and her insistence on their testifying to this and that.

'It's somewhere in Piazza Signoria . . .'

The Marshal opened his mouth and shut it again. There weren't that many restaurants in Piazza della Signoria. It was quicker to go and ask there. He banged his hat on and stumped off through the courtyard, muttering, 'I'll give her testify . . .'

It turned out to be the restaurant nearest to the Palazzo Vecchio. There was only one couple lingering over coffee and cigarettes. All the other tables had been cleared and had clean white cloths on them. The head waiter was putting his coat on. The Marshal found his man sweeping up in the kitchen. He was as surly and unprepossessing as his wife and about half her size. To avoid losing his temper the Marshal said it himself along with his first question: 'It was the morning that it snowed . . .' He was prepared for a battle if the porter turned out to be as difficult a customer as his wife. He needn't have worried.

'I remember. Yes, I did open the door for somebody when I was leaving for work. It's unusual for anybody to ring at that time. I thought perhaps it was the postman come early. My wife was in the bathroom.'

'Who was it?'

'I've no idea. Nobody came in so perhaps it was a mistake. I was going out anyway and I was a bit surprised to find nobody there.'

'You didn't do anything about it?'

'What should I have done if there was nobody there? To tell you the truth, I thought it was probably one of those Sardinian beggars with their bagpipes. There was one of them on the other side of the street. I wouldn't have opened up if I'd known; they're a thieving bunch and they usually work in pairs. I thought it was probably the other one who had rung, on the cadge.'

'But you never actually saw the other one?'

'No, I told you. There was nobody there when I came out.'

'What time was it?'

'Eight o'clock.'

'How long after pressing the door switch did you come outside?'

'A few minutes. I don't know. The time it took to put my coat on and pick up my keys and stuff.'

As simple as that. And he, too, had remarked on the one piper. The Marshal decided it was time to pay a visit to Headquarters. Before he left he asked: 'What's your full name?'

'Bertelli, Sergio.'

'I'll need a written statement from you later. If you didn't think of mentioning this caller to your wife, didn't it even occur to you to mention it to us when you heard what had happened?'

'Nothing happened that I know of. Why should I have told you?'

'You don't know that a tenant from your building was kidnapped that morning and that the evidence you've just given could be vital?'

'I don't know anything of the sort.'

There was no point in asking if his wife hadn't told him if they never spoke.

'Don't you read the papers?'

'Only the sports page.'

'And you didn't even notice that a tenant from the first floor is missing?'

'I know nothing about the tenants. That's my wife's job.'

'"I am not in the least racist. I don't object to these people on grounds of race and I don't believe that any other Florentine does either. All we ask of anyone coming to live in a civilized city is that they accept the code of behaviour of civilized, decent people'' etcetera, etcetera . . . The ones that start off with ''I'm not racist but'' are always the most racially prejudiced.'

'True.' The Substitute flipped open the latest of the pile of newspapers on the Captain's desk. 'Another three letters . . . But the editor declares the correspondence closed. So much the better.'

The polemic in the newspapers had begun not over the kidnapping but over a fight that had broken out a few days previously in a bar much frequented by the young Sardinians who hung around the city and by the city gangs who sold them drugs. No one knew what the quarrel had been about and no one cared. In recent months the residents of the area around the bar had been complaining almost nightly to the police about the noise that went on until the small hours and about the hypodermics left strewn around the piazza, a serious health hazard to the children who played there during the day. The fight, in which one Sardinian had slit another's throat from ear to ear without succeeding in killing him, had been the last straw and had resulted in an unprecedented outburst of anti-Sardinian feeling that involved not just the affected area but the whole city. The 'Sardinian problem' became the chief subject of conversation in every bar, drawing-room and noble palace in the city.

What I say is, if they want to live here they should live like us, not sleep outside on that mountain like animals.

I never realized there were any that near, I thought they were all in the Mugello region . . .

I remember when my husband was alive and we had a Sardinian couple with some unpronounceable name and it took me three months to teach her to make tea properly. I don't think she ever let the water boil.

I had an aunt who rented a field to a shepherd. The one who left me that brooch you always liked. So simpatico, *I thought. I was only about ten. He used to pay with cheese . . .*

Lorenzo was in Sardinia last month. He wanted to see Garibaldi's house. He gets so easily depressed that I'm happy if anything will distract him.

You should suggest he visit Portugal. Italy wouldn't have any of the problems she has if the King were still here.

Few people mentioned the kidnapping. There had been nothing about it on the television news since the day the car was found.

'Who's the man they arrested for the throat-slitting?' The Substitute lit a cigar and began to fold the newspaper neatly and rapidly.

'Garau. A regular customer of ours. Very shifty.'

'He's not on your list of suspects?'

'Frankly, apart from Antonio Demontis, the terrible brother, who's being watched, we don't have any real suspects—though I'd very much like to know where Piladu's son and Scano's boy have got to. There's a young plain-clothes man working on it but he has to go slowly. He's infiltrated the group and is buying regular small doses but he can't start asking questions too soon.'

'Is it the same bar?'

'As the stabbing? Yes, but they all go there.'

'Not much chance of finding out what that fight was about?'

'None whatever. And still nothing from the Consulate. No contact.'

'Do you think she's dead?'

'Not yet . . .'

'What about the Nilsen girl?'

'If anything, she's more nervous since she came out of hospital. Probably she feels more at risk. It's not easy to take up your life again when it's been so brutally interrupted. She's still in regular contact with Sub-lieutenant Bacci and I have every hope that he'll gain her confidence.'

After considering this aspect of the case for some moments the Substitute remarked: 'You chose your man well.'

'Yes. His English is excellent and he's very conscientious.'

The Substitute hid the faintest of smiles by drawing very deliberately on his cigar.

The Adjutant knocked and came in.

'Sub-lieutenant Bacci to see you, sir.'

'Send him in.'

As Bacci emerged through the blue fog that had collected near the door it occurred to the Captain that if Fusarri had been the normal sort of Substitute he would have had to go and report to him at his office, leaving his own smoke-free. But by this time the Captain had grown used to living in a blue haze. He motioned the young officer to sit down.

'You have something for me?'

'Yes. I've had to piece it together over the last three days. The information only came out bit by bit since she's still not easy in her mind about talking to us. I suppose she's afraid of anything happening to her friend as a result. I'm not even sure if what I've managed to get will be all that useful . . .'

'Go on.'

'Well, they were blindfolded before they got out of their own car that morning, as you know. Even so, I thought it was worth persisting, trying to get her to remember noises, smells, anything that would give us a clue to where they were taken. It seems that when they were made to lie down in the back of the truck and their hands were tied behind them, Katrine remembers there being rags underneath her. Some of them smelt of oil or grease of a kind she didn't recognize. I gave her a few samples from the labs without telling her what they were and she picked out gun oil as being the nearest. It was almost sure to be, of course, out in the country and at this time of year. Almost everyone hunts. But there were also some other rags, a sort of muslin, she thought, very soft but with stiff patches and it stank of bad meat. So much so that she remembers trying to wriggle her face away from it without success. I still thought it meant the truck was used for hunting but I asked the labs to check her clothing just in case. They had already found what I was looking for, traces of gun oil, some brown dog hairs and minute traces of dead flesh.'

'It's what you'd find in the back of any van out in the country, as you said.'

'Except that they say it's certainly not game but butcher's meat. They'll be able to tell us for certain later. They think it's lamb.'

'That sounds too obvious to be true.'

'Nevertheless, that's what they say.'

'And anything on where they were taken?'

'Definitely not up the mountain. They went all the way by car and she doesn't think they were on the road very long. Maybe about a quarter of an hour. They seemed to keep up a fairly regular speed and, although it was bumpy, she's sure they didn't climb any steep hills in a low gear. When they got out they were taken inside a building and made to sit on a stone floor that was gritty and unswept. They hadn't negotiated any furniture to get to the far side of the room and sit against the opposite wall and she had the impression, either because of that or because of the resonance of voices, that the room was empty. Once they were on the floor their feet were bound and somebody was left on guard beside them. Somebody who prodded them occasionally, she thinks with a rifle as he wasn't right up close, to make sure they realized he was there. They weren't hurt or threatened verbally—in fact, apart from the message she was given they weren't spoken to at all. There were two men apart from the one with the rifle and she heard them quarrelling for a long time in another room.'

'Does she have any idea what the quarrel was about?'

'She couldn't understand or even hear them all that well. Even so, she felt sure that it was something to do with her, that there should only have been the Maxwell girl there. One of the men sounded furious, the other frightened—the one who'd been in their car. It was only guesswork on her part, naturally, but it's more than probable that she's right. She didn't normally stay the night with her friend. She had no reason to since her own flat is within walking distance. Whoever did the planning on this job couldn't have expected to find a second person getting into the car.'

'And just why did she stay the night in Piazza Pitti?'

'I still haven't been able to find out for sure. She's quite vague, even evasive about it. I keep on asking but she's given me three different answers up to now; that Deborah felt a bit depressed, that they'd been out very late to the last show at the cinema in Via Romana which is very near to Piazza Pitti.'

'That's also true, we have the tickets. And the third reason?'

'Even vaguer. She'd heard stories about people being attacked and their handbags stolen and so decided not to walk across town alone. Not that that's unreasonable in itself but it never seems to have bothered her before since she says herself she didn't normally stay the night, even if they'd been out late.'

'They're not contradictory stories, of course,' said the Captain slowly.

'I know, and they're probably all true in their way, but I'm sure there's something else that she's not telling me . . .'

'You think there may have been something wrong with the Maxwell girl? My men have questioned everyone in her class at the school. Nothing came out, but then she seems to have been very secretive. Nobody got very close to her.'

'Katrine was closer to her than anybody and very fond of her. I'm sure that if there is anything she'll tell me once she gets her confidence back.'

'Then keep questioning her. At the moment she's our only hope.'

'Should I go tomorrow as usual . . .?' The young man's eyes kept involuntarily catching those of the Substitute, who was staring at him pleasantly.

'Why do you ask?' The significance of the Substitute's earlier remark was gradually dawning on the Captain. 'If you mean because it's your day off, there are no days off during this case unless I decide I can spare you.'

'It wasn't that . . . only that it's Palm Sunday . . . I was just wondering if I could change the timetable of my visit but it isn't important . . .' He couldn't say what he wanted to say in front of the Substitute.

'Any change in routine could be enough to undermine Signorina Nilsen's confidence.' He emphasized the surname slightly, knowing he was being unfair because they hadn't known it during those first days when Bacci had sat by her bedside. He let the young man go and was relieved that the telephone rang before the Substitute could speak.

'Yes?'

'Sentry room, sir. Visitors for you. The American Consul General and a Mr Maxwell.'

CHAPTER 8

There was also a Mrs Maxwell. Beside her tall, plump husband she looked even smaller than she was. Her perfume immediately overpowered the tobacco fumes, her coat was of pale chamois leather and the silk scarf knotted over it bore a conspicuous signature.

It was significant that it was the Consul General who spoke first. There was no outburst of parental panic. It meant that they had already discussed the problem at length and decided what line to take. It was evidently to be a very reserved one. The Consul General addressed himself exclusively to the Substitute in slow, accurate Italian, pronounced with his native accent.

'It took us some time to trace Mr Maxwell since his business interests take him all over the States. Fortunately, it happens that we have a common friend and both he and Mr Maxwell were to be at a board meeting in New York on Monday.'

'On Monday . . .' repeated the Substitute, as if wanting to take this piece of information in very particularly. He leaned forward with a sudden movement, politely offered round cigarettes and cigars, and then sat back as though retiring from the proceedings to his usual position of observer. 'Captain Maestrangelo,' he said, filling his pipe rapidly and efficiently, 'needs to know something about the family, everything about the family, in fact, and quickly.' He didn't look at any of them.

The Captain filled the space provided for him, speaking first to the Consul General.

'Perhaps you would tell Mr Maxwell that you will translate my questions for him and that he may speak directly to me in English. We'll waste less time that way. I'd like to know the condition of the family, where and how they live, what his relations with his daughter were like and whether she had any particular problems.'

Maxwell's voice was rather high-pitched and soft, but despite this he spoke with the authority of someone accustomed to getting his own way.

'I have a number of houses in various parts of the United States. We spend time in all of them, depending on the season and on where we feel like being.'

'These properties are investments? Or do you need them because of working in various parts of the country?'

The Consul General translated. Maxwell evaded the first part of the question. 'They're well away from the places my work takes me to. They're not anything extravagant, don't get me wrong. Some of them, like for instance the farm in Connecticut, are quite small. If I like a place I buy it. I guess you could say it's a hobby. We like to lend them to friends of ours.'

'But not to sell them?'

'If I feel like a change, I don't see what this has to do with my daughter.'

'A friend of your daughter's gave us to understand that you lived in Michigan.'

'Debbie was born there and we still have a place there, but not the same one that she grew up in. I sold that when I remarried.'

'Is your first wife dead?'

'We're divorced. She remarried more or less at the same time as I did. She married a banker from Charlestown, West Virginia, and that's where they live.'

'How old was your daughter when you divorced?'

'She'd be about fifteen.'

'Does she still keep in touch with her mother?'

'Not an awful lot. They wrote one another at first but then my ex-wife had another child, you know how it is . . .'

'Your ex-wife is somewhat younger than you are?'

'Eight years.'

'Do you think it's possible that your daughter may be very unhappy?'

'I'm perfectly sure she's not.'

'The divorce didn't upset her?'

'She's gotten over all that. She's almost twenty.'

'Would it not have been more usual for your daughter to have stayed with her mother?'

'Jean didn't give me much warning. I came back from a business trip to find her gone.'

'Leaving your daughter alone?'

'Debbie was in boarding-school.'

'And in the holidays?'

'She had a choice of houses to go to in those days.'

'But no home?'

'Excuse me?'

'Did you spend the holidays with her?'

'I spent time with her, sure I spent time with her. Just where is all this leading us? You seem to me to be wasting an awful lot of time.'

'I'm sorry if my questions disturb you. I'm trying to find out what sort of emotional state your daughter has been in over the past six months. You don't live in this country and don't do business here. Your daughter doesn't live extravagantly enough for it to be noticed that she has more money than the average student. Whoever decided she was worth kidnapping got their information from your daughter herself.'

'What would Debbie be doing mixing with criminals?'

'That's what I would like to know. Did she ever use drugs?'

'She did not!'

Maxwell's face had darkened and his wife was looking at him anxiously as if she would like to interfere. She even murmured, almost inaudibly: 'Don't you think . . .'

But her husband interrupted her.

'I do the talking, Dorothy. Debbie is my daughter.'

The Captain continued mildly: 'I understand your daughter is here to study?'

'That is correct.'

'Why isn't she at college in America?'

'She wanted to come to Italy.'

'Over twenty American colleges have branches here in Florence.'

'There doesn't seem to me to be anything wrong with the school she's in now.'

'Most of the students are postgraduates.'

'Debbie . . . Debbie dropped out of college after the first year.'

'Why? Did something go wrong?'

'Nothing went wrong! She just changed her mind.'

'In which of your many houses did you spend Christmas, Mr Maxwell?'

'My wife and I spent Christmas in the Bahamas.'

'Did your daughter go with you?'

'We invited Debbie.'

'But she didn't go?'

'No, she didn't.'

'Her friends were under the impression that she was to spend Christmas with you in America.'

'We talked about it, but then at the last minute we thought of the Bahamas. My wife and I like to travel. We invited Debbie to join us but she'd had an invitation from a girlfriend to spend Christmas in Norway and she decided to take that invitation up. So I guess it worked out OK. She had a wonderful time.'

'Did you meet this friend when you came over here after Christmas?'

'We did not. Of course, we were here for only a short time and what time we had we spent with Debbie. Dorothy had a lot of shopping to do and my daughter took a little time off school to take us around.'

'Did you ever worry about your daughter's living alone in a city?'

'Come on now, this isn't New York.'

'Your daughter was kidnapped at gunpoint.'

'And apparently she wasn't alone. Debbie knew how to defend herself, I saw to that, but a kidnapping's something else.'

'What exactly do you mean by "defend herself"?'

'In America the police in major cities run courses that teach women to defend themselves, particularly against rape.'

'Your daughter followed one of these courses?'

'She most certainly did. I insisted on it.'

'Why?'

'Why . . .? Because she intended to come over here was one reason. She took the course last summer before leaving the States.'

'But, as you yourself said, this is not New York.'

'You seem to have your share of crime. And those instructors aren't joking, believe me. They really teach them how to hurt.'

'So I've heard.' Though he'd never really believed that any woman would behave that coldly and that violently in response to an attack. Experience told him that a woman's natural instinct was to defend herself rather than to hurt the attacker. And in the recent article he had read on the subject, even the sergeant in charge of the course had not believed that any woman would take his one piece of infallible advice. They preferred their little aerosols of teargas which gave them a false sense of security. He let the matter drop.

'Do you own any property in this country, Mr Maxwell?'

'I do not.'

'How many times have you been over here?'

'Our visit to Debbie this year was only my second time in Italy.'

'When was the first time?'

'Before Debbie was born. I brought my first wife to Naples as part of our honeymoon.'

'What exactly is your business, Mr Maxwell?'

'I'm a major shareholder in a number of companies and consequently a director of them. They're spread all over the country, which is why I have to travel so much and why the Consulate had difficulty tracing me.'

'Do you consider yourself a rich man?'

'Not as rich as some.'

'But you would be able to pay the ransom without difficulty, assuming the money was allowed into the country?'

'I think you can let me worry about that.'

'Unfortunately I have to worry about it too. Strictly speaking, you would be aiding and abetting—'

'Now listen, you can't stop me from rescuing my own daughter!'

The Consul General would have given a great deal to stop this exchange going any further but he could hardly say anything without worsening the situation for himself.

'We, too, have every intention of rescuing your daughter,' the Captain said mildly, 'but we would also like to catch the people who kidnapped her. Kidnapping is a business and a very profitable one. The more profitable you help to make it, the more people will be kidnapped in the future.'

'I don't care about other people being kidnapped, that's your problem. I want my daughter back alive and if the price is one and a—'

The Captain relaxed and the Substitute sat up again. It was the latter who, ignoring the red-faced Maxwell whose wife was holding on to his arm, asked the Consul General:

'When did you receive the message?'

'Eight days ago.' The Consul shot an annoyed glance at Maxwell for making a fool of him.

'Eight days ago,' repeated the Substitute in the same way as he had repeated "On Monday". He didn't even ask the next question but went on looking at the Consul General expectantly.

'It was a personal message for Mr Maxwell. You surely must realize that I couldn't take the responsibility . . . if anything should have happened to his daughter . . .'

'Something might well have happened to her after eight days. When did you miss your daughter, Mr Maxwell?'

'Naturally, when the call came from the Consulate.'

'In other words, you didn't miss her. We have been looking for her for three weeks. Captain . . .' He selected a fresh cigar and sat back.

'What was the exact wording of the message?'

'*Mr Maxwell, we have Deborah. The price is one and a half milliardi*. We couldn't make any decision on Mr Maxwell's behalf.'

'I understand. Were you told where to leave the money?'

'No, nothing else.'

The Captain believed him. Until the kidnappers knew that Maxwell had the money ready they wouldn't name a place. At any rate, they had known that the Nilsen girl hadn't delivered her message unless they were guessing, word having got around that she had been picked up unconscious. He turned to Maxwell.

'You could still cooperate with us.'

'I just want my daughter.'

'I see. We shall, of course, cooperate with you.'

'What do you mean by that?'

'How do you know these people really have your daughter?'

'She is missing, isn't she? And there's the message, not to mention the other girl who was a witness!'

'To her having been kidnapped, yes. But that was three weeks ago, as the Substitute Prosecutor has already pointed out to you. Where she is now, in whose hands, whether she's still alive, these are the questions you need to have answered before paying a ransom.'

The colour left Maxwell's face. Was the reality of the situation only just getting through to him?

'I've no way of knowing that,' he said more quietly. 'I can't take the risk . . .'

'We have ways of finding out, and we will cooperate with you as I said, regardless of whether you choose to help us. When the next phone call comes, which it will very shortly, you will ask for a copy of that day's newspaper signed by your daughter. You will also ask for the answers to three questions.'

'What questions?' By now he was quite subdued.

'Any questions you like provided that you know only your daughter can answer them; the nickname of a childhood friend, for example, or the description of some pet she used to have, anything that she will know and her captors can't know. Think it over. When you have the newspaper and the three answers you will at least know that your daughter is still alive and in a fit state to respond. In the meantime . . .' He drew the folded note from the file on his desk. 'This letter was given to the girl who was released. We don't know for certain but it was probably to be given to you on your arrival.'

Maxwell examined the letter in silence, let the Consul General read it and then put it back into the Captain's open hand. He still showed little emotional reaction though he was evidently angry with himself for letting his natural arrogance be so easily quashed.

The Captain turned to Mrs Maxwell: 'Do you get on well with your stepdaughter.'

'We get along just fine. Of course, we've never seen all that much of each other . . .'

'When you went shopping together here, did she ever say anything about the way in which she usually spent her allowance?'

'Why, no . . . I suppose she bought clothes like other girls, and went out and enjoyed herself. I'm sure she has lots of friends.'

'She has no health problem that you know of?'

'None at all, she's a strong girl . . . Back home she used to love riding. She couldn't ride here, of course, being in town, that's why John . . .'

'Yes?'

'I think he would have liked her to come home.' She looked anxiously at her husband.

It was she who, just before they left, showed signs of being seriously upset.

'They won't harm her . . . you understand what I mean . . . they won't touch her . . .?' Her face had become blotchy under her make-up and her eyes were suddenly filling up.

'It's very unlikely. Kidnapping is a business, as I told your husband. These people have nothing personal against the victim. It's in their interests to keep her safe. She won't be comfortable but she'll be properly fed and cared for. Before you go, would you mind telling me where you're staying?'

'At the Excelsior.'

'The stubborn type, our Mr Maxwell,' remarked the Substitute once he and the Captain were alone again. 'Though it didn't seem to surprise you. Is that sort of behaviour normal?'

'It's certainly not unusual. Mothers are a great deal more help once they've calmed down and been told what to do. But then it's probably a case of ignorance is bliss. There are very few fathers of kidnap victims who aren't worried about their financial affairs being looked at too closely. The idea that someone has already taken a very close look before choosing the victim shakes them considerably. I doubt if this man is an exception.'

'He took his time getting here, too, if he was informed on Monday. Today's Saturday. We don't know when he arrived in Florence, of course . . .'

The Captain picked up the external phone.

'Get me the Excelsior hotel, will you . . . no, I'll hang on . . . Excelsior? Could you tell me if Mr John Maxwell has arrived yet . . . Wednesday lunchtime. Thank you.' He turned a pencil over and over between his fingers. 'What difference could a day or two make?'

'Not trouble finding a seat on a plane, I imagine. First class and in March.'

The telephone rang.

'Marshal Guarnaccia at Pitti for you, sir.'

'Thank you. Good afternoon, Marshal.'

'I was coming over to see you but things have happened. First of all I managed to talk to Bertelli, the husband of the weeping woman at number three. He works in a restaurant. It was he who let the kidnapper in before he left for work. His wife was in the bathroom. He noticed the one bagpiper like I did, and what I say is that we were meant to. I don't believe it was a coincidence, and if it wasn't—' he had finally sorted it out—'if it wasn't then it means that Sardinian shepherds dressed themselves up as Sardinian shepherds to do a kidnapping. It's more ridiculous than a coincidence. Somebody's trying to make sure we blame the Sardinians.'

The Captain had as good as said the same himself about the traces of lamb's meat in the truck.

'Even so, Demontis is Sardinian and so are Piladu and Scano's boy.'

'Wait a minute, I'm coming to that. Piladu's son—he's dead. That's why I've been delayed in getting over to see you. I intended to pick up my car and come over to see you as soon as I'd talked to Bertelli, but when I got back here Lorenzini had this message from up near the fort. Some children spotted the feet sticking out of the bushes by the roadside. It's in my Quarter, of course—I don't know how long he's been dead but I went up there and the doctor was still there. He said it's almost certainly an overdose. They've taken the body over to the Medico-Legal Institute. I've only just come back down.'

'You'd better come over here, anyway.'

'If we're going out to Pontino I'll have to warn my Brigadier.'

'I think we'll have to.'

The Marshal roared into the distance for Lorenzini and then said: 'It looks as if this might have nothing to do with the kidnapping.'

'I'm not sure.'

'It could have something to do with that fight in the bar, though. I'll come over, then.' He rang off.

'Piladu's son's been found dead.'

'What of?'

'Probably an overdose.'

'Who'll tell his father?'

'I suppose the Brigadier out at Pontino had better. I want to go out there.' He rang for his adjutant and sent him to bring Bacci back.

'In that case I'll go over to the Procura. You still think this boy was involved in our case?'

'Yes, I do.'

'I thought so. I'll get over there before they appoint another Substitute to look into it.'

'I suppose you should, though I imagine Guarnaccia will have mentioned it.'

'Hm. Incidentally, I've been reading some recent studies of Sardinian banditry. It seems this sort of thing's been going on ever since the Romans colonized Sardinia and drove the indigenous population of the rich pasture in the lowlands up into the Barbagia.'

'Yes, it has.' But when did the Substitute find time for his leisurely reading? He always seemed to be on the move . . .

'And they say they still call themselves "Pelliti" because they used to dress only in goat and sheep skins.'

'And send us violent political messages about freeing Sardinia from Italian rule, while investing their ransom money in land and building speculation in the south of France and even South America.'

'They only stole sheep from the Romans.'

'Sheep make a noise. People, if you point a gun at them, don't.'

CHAPTER 9

'Things aren't as they should be, of course . . .' The Brigadier had at last found an appreciative audience, and he and the Marshal bounced along together comfortably in the jeep with the Captain and Bacci following in a car. 'We've been without a Marshal nearly four months—not that I can't cope, but you know how it is when half the boys you get are on National Service and by the time you've begun to knock them into shape they're ready to leave.'

The Marshall grunted.

'When I think how it was when I joined up . . . you're not so badly off down in Florence where at least you've got a central canteen, but ever since we've had to do without a resident housekeeper in the smaller stations we've had to spend half our time teaching mothers' boys to cook pasta.'

'Mmph . . .'

'It's one thing if you're fully-staffed but if you think that whichever of my boys is on guard duty for the day is responsible for the shopping as well as the cooking, and I have to put another boy on guard as substitute to him and another at the disposition of the local magistrate, and I've two out on motor-bike patrol—where am I when a case like this comes up and I've got to be out?'

'It's difficult . . .'

'I'll say it's difficult. How many men do they think I've got?'

'How many have you?'

'I've got enough just to manage, but things aren't what they should be and it's not what we were used to in the old days.'

'Ah no . . .'

'Not that a case like this comes up every day, I'm not saying that and I'm not saying I can't cope, but it should be a Marshal on this job so that I'm there if anything comes up in the village, you see what I mean?'

The Marshal grunted.

'I've said as much—though not in so many words—to the Captain, for all the good it does, but you understand what I'm talking about. This is Piladu's place, but if you ask me there'll be nobody in at this hour on a Saturday. Not until he comes home to milk . . . There'll be nobody in at this hour!' he repeated loudly, to the men behind as he got down from the jeep.

Car doors slammed and chickens scattered.

'What about his wife?' asked the Captain.

'It's Saturday,' repeated the Brigadier patiently. 'She'll be doing her weekend shopping.'

They fell silent for a moment, all of them wondering if she was shopping for the son who was lying in a dissecting trench at the Medico-Legal Institute.

'He hadn't been home for weeks, anyway . . .' The Brigadier continued their common thought aloud. 'At least, he hadn't if they were telling the truth.' It wasn't likely that they had been. The boy was almost sure to have been home at intervals, if only for a change of clothing.

'We don't know how long he's been dead,' murmured the Marshal, 'though it couldn't have been long, he wasn't . . .'

'What time do you think she'll be back?' interrupted the Captain, addressing the Brigadier.

'About half past six, I should think. In time to put her shopping away before he brings the milk in. He'll be back first . . .' He looked at his watch. 'It's almost six.'

The sun had already lost its warmth and the light had faded just a little, giving the empty farmhouse and its ramshackle outbuildings a forlorn look. Bacci and the Marshal were staring in at the uncurtained window below the steps that led to the front door. They could make out stands of wooden shelving in the gloom, the nearest cheeses a luminous white, the furthest ones matured to a dark, oily yellow.

'Good many hours of work gone into that lot,' the Marshal said quietly.

'"Many the rich cheeses I pressed for ungrateful townsfolk,
Yet never did I get home with much money in my pocket,"'

quoted Bacci, who had studied at the Liceo Classico.

The Marshall gave him a funny look. 'Pecorino costs ten thousand lire a kilo.'

'But if you allow for a middleman . . .'

'They sell it directly to the shops!'

'He's here.' The Brigadier had heard the faint tinkle of sheepbells and the distant bark of the younger dog.

The black figure came into view against a jostling white drift. The old dog plodded alongside while the younger one careered wildly up and down without managing to distract the sheep who were eager to get home and be relieved of their milk.

Piladu was carrying a newborn lamb that seemed to be hanging lifelessly under his arm. When he got close enough they saw that its hind legs were twitching feebly. He knew that four of them wouldn't come for anything he might have done. There was no need to ask what it was about. It was the Brigadier he looked at.

'You've arrested him?' But they wouldn't come just to tell him that either. 'He's dead?'

'Yes.'

The sheep were pushing into the fold, stumbling and bleating. The younger son was coming along in the distance, taking big strides with the help of an overlong crook.

'Ruff, Fido, ruff, get on . . .' said Piladu, without taking his eyes from the four men in uniform. The dog moved off a few paces and turned back, wagging his tail anxiously. 'Get on,' Piladu repeated, and the dog walked round to the back of the sheepfold. 'Was it an overdose?'

'Probably. There'll have to be . . . We'll be able to tell you for certain later.'

'It makes no difference, does it? He's dead.'

Things would get worse, not better, when his wife arrived. If it was worth asking they might as well ask now.

'This business of him going missing . . .' began the Brigadier, 'It's possible that he might have been involved in something big. If you know anything about it at all, now that—If you can tell us anything it might save a young girl's life.'

'It's his mother's fault . . . She ruined him . . .' He was lifting up the lamb's head, pulling on its muzzle to make it bleat. 'She ruined him because he was her first. If I'd had my way . . .' One of the sheep pushed its way out of the flock in response to the lamb's feeble noise. He went and laid the limp creature down on a tuft of grass near the fold to let its mother lick it.

'You could save this girl's life. It's too late to protect

your lad, but you could still help her . . .

Piladu took a baby's bottle from somewhere inside his cloak. 'Too weak to do for itself.' He crouched behind the mother to squirt milk into the bottle. 'She ruined him and now he's dead.' His face was turned from them.

'Will you help us find out what happened?'

Piladu kept his face averted, staring over the heads of his lamenting flock. He might have been talking to the sheep when he said softly:

'God damn the lot of you.'

'Young ones today won't stand for it. They'd sooner take a job eight to five in a factory, if they can get it, and the worst of it is that the ones who do take it on can't find a wife. When his younger son comes of an age when he wants to get married, any girl he brings home is going to take one look at the life his mother has to put up with and she'll be off.'

'That's true . . .'

'Of course it's true but where's it all going to end? If nobody wants to work the land—we'll go round by the villa. Are they following behind? They are. It's tragic—there's a chap along this road that I like to keep my eye on and it's as long as it's short—to lose your eldest boy. He was never a help to his father, but even so . . . It doesn't bear thinking about.'

The Marshal was thinking about his own two sons. How could anybody get over a thing like that? And the mother . . .

'Doesn't bear thinking about,' The Brigadier said again, repeatedly lifting and pushing back his hat, though he had it on perfectly straight. 'There are times when this job gets you down. Nobody wants to tell a man his eldest son's gone. Sometimes I'd sooner be doing some other job. Now, who's that? That's somebody who's up to no good . . . I'd recognize that slinking walk anywhere.

Now, what's he doing round here?' He stuck his arm out of the open side of the jeep and stamped a big boot on the brake.

To their left, a figure had slipped between the trees that lined the driveway leading to the villa.

'I wonder if he saw us?'

'I don't see how he could have done. He had his back to us and other things on his mind by the look of him. Who is it?'

'That's Scano's boy, that's who that is. A lad we'd like to talk to, the Captain and I.' He stuck his head out to look behind. The Captain's car had stopped. There was no room to draw alongside.

'I'd better have a word,' said the Brigadier, withdrawing his head and opening the door.

The Captain wound down his window, baffled.

'I've just spotted Scano's boy,' explained the Brigadier.

'I didn't see anyone.'

'You wouldn't be able to from behind me. He was heading for the villa but not on the drive itself. He evidently didn't want to be seen.'

'How did you know? Why did you come this way?'

'I didn't know anything. I came this way—it's as long as it's short—because of Pratesi and his sausage factory.'

'Because of . . .?'

'Because of Pratesi. We'll pass his place in a minute. It's nothing to do with this job, I just like to drive past whenever I can because sooner or later I'll catch him at it. I can't prove anything yet but he's not just making sausages, he's got some racket going buying and selling stuff on the side and the money's not going through his books. Anyway, Scano's boy must have been going to see the gamekeeper at the villa.'

'The gamekeeper? What about that young shepherd we saw there the other day, what was his name?'

'Rudolfo? No no no, he wasn't going there, you can't

get there, not from the main drive. There's a wall dividing the villa and gardens from the paddock and stables that Rudolfo uses. There's a door in it but that's been kept padlocked since the family doesn't come any more. You can only get to Rudolfo's by the road we took the other day when they found the car—or else on foot there's a bit of a patch half a kilometre on from here—and in any case Rudolfo won't be down until tomorrow, being Palm Sunday. No. It's the gamekeeper he's going to see. What should we do?'

'Your men know this area best. Get one of them out here in plain clothes and on a civilian motor-bike—better still a moped, it looks more innocent. And tell him to keep on the move.'

From the Brigadier's office the Captain telephoned Maxwell at the Excelsior, sending Bacci through to the communicating duty room to pick up the phone there.

'Has there been a further message from them?' He nodded at Bacci for a translation.

Maxwell hesitated before saying: 'Yes, there has . . .'

'Where?'

'Where . . .?'

'Through the Consulate?'

'I—I'm not prepared to say.'

'They telephoned you at your hotel, didn't they?'

Silence.

'How did they know where you were staying?'

'That's no secret, anybody could have found that out!'

'Mr Maxwell, I understand only too well that you would like to pay this ransom as quickly as possible and take no risks and that since I want to catch these kidnappers, we are working at cross purposes to a certain extent. Nevertheless, unless there's some cooperation between us, your daughter could lose her life. You need the help I can give you because if you unknowingly make a false move or fail to react promptly because you're not sure what to do, your daughter will be dispensed with as being too risky a property. She is valuable to them but her value has its limits. They assume you will get help and advice from me. The risk of having you talk to me is balanced by my preventing you from blundering or delaying. They know that, unless I am very fortunate, the only chance I'll have to catch them is the moment in which they take the ransom, and they know equally well that you won't risk your daughter's life by telling me where that's going to happen.'

'You could have me followed.'

'And you could send someone else whom I don't know. I'm sure you've already agreed to do that.'

Another silence. The Captain and Bacci looked at each other through the communicating door. Dealing through a third party made things more difficult than they were already but the young officer couldn't deal with a situation like this and the Captain couldn't risk not making himself perfectly understood. When Maxwell still didn't answer he went on more gently:

'Please try and remember that I didn't create the situation you're in but I do have more experience of it than you do. For reasons it would be too complicated to explain to you now, I believe that this may not be a professional kidnapping and that the people concerned are inefficient and very probably frightened. Had it been a professional job all that would matter from your point of view would be that you followed their instructions and moved at their pace with my help. As it is, I think every hour that passes increases the risk of your not seeing your daughter again whether you pay the ransom or not, and that by paying you may well be signing her death warrant. Consequently, if you don't feel you want to cooperate with me I shall be justified in going ahead with my job and in leaving you free to act in any way you think fit.'

'Leaving me free?'

'To take whatever line you like, yes.'

'And then what do I do when I get the answer to these questions you told me to ask, and the newspaper?'

'That's for you to decide. You may want to take the advice of your Consulate.'

'I may just do that—I'm going to call the Consul General right now!' He hung up.

After sending Bacci off to get himself a coffee from the Brigadier who was losing his patience with a recruit in the kitchen, the Captain shut out the noise and sat down to wait, glancing now and then at his watch. He would have liked to telephone Marshal Guarnaccia who had gone back down to Florence but he didn't want to block the line, and in any case the Marshal had said something about going to the prison. It wasn't that the Captain had anything specific to ask him, but on the few occasions they had worked together the Marshal had always had something helpful to offer. The only trouble was that although he never missed a trick, he was dreadfully slow. If you asked him a question you might not get an answer for a week. The Captain knew that he hadn't got a week. For all he knew, he might already be too late.

When a quarter of an hour had passed the Brigadier poked his head round the door, wondering if the Captain had gone off somewhere, it was so quiet. He muttered something inaudible and withdrew. Half an hour passed.

At the end of the case, if everything went well, a relieved John Maxwell would thank him profusely and hug his daughter for the television cameras. With small children it was simpler. There were fewer tensions, and in their lives not so many things had had time to go wrong. At the end of the case people would see a bit of film of the child sitting on the drawing-room sofa between his parents who never took their eyes from him during the interview.

'Who was it who rescued you, do you know?'

'The Carabinieri.'

'When did you realize what was happening? Did you see someone in uniform?'

'No. The first man who came in was in ordinary clothes. Then I saw the uniforms.'

'And you knew you were safe?'

'Yes.'

There were no television cameras now. He looked at his watch. Forty minutes. It rarely took more than an hour. Sometimes he would have liked to unburden himself to somebody, but his officers and men had their own problems. The only person who came to mind was the Substitute, but years of battling with arrogant, ambitious magistrates had taken their toll and he smiled ruefully at himself for having such a peculiar idea. Well, later he would telephone Guarnaccia . . . just to keep him informed.

The Captain closed his eyes. Patience. It rarely took more than an hour.

It took an hour and ten minutes. The telephone rang. It was Mrs Maxwell who spoke, not her husband.

'We rang your own number but they gave us this one . . .'

The extra ten minutes had probably only been the time it had taken them to find him. Judging from her voice, she had been crying.

'I talked to my husband and we feel there's something we should have mentioned that might just be important . . . Can you understand me?'

'I understand you.' It was their turn to do the talking; he would manage better without Bacci now.

'We didn't think of it before . . . and it's not something

John likes to talk about. You do understand? I do hope you won't be angry.'

'No, Signora, I won't be angry.'

'Debbie . . . Well, there was some trouble at college and she had to leave.'

'Drugs?'

'Only marijuana, not what you'd really call drugs. In some places in the States it's legal now so we didn't think we—'

'How long ago?'

'Excuse me?'

'How long ago? The marijuana?'

'About a year ago. She was only in college the one year, less than a year if you—we just wondered if she tried to buy some here, that's all, and that could be how she might have met the wrong kind of people. It's not legal here?'

'No.'

'Well, we thought we should just mention it.'

'Is your husband there?'

'He's right here beside me. We'll do all we can—'

'Signora, thank you. I would like to speak to your husband, please.' It was better that way than making him ask. The important thing now was to let him save face. The Captain filled in the space where Maxwell might have thought he had to apologize, and then asked him quickly: 'What did you do in the north of Italy in January? Skiing? Please don't answer without thinking. You stayed in a hotel, I think?'

And filled in a registration form that could be checked on.

'I had a business deal to complete in Turin.' The Captain said nothing so that he felt obliged to go on, to explain himself. 'I know I told you that was my first visit since my honeymoon with Debbie's mother and that's true. I don't do business over here, this was an exception.'

'Wait a moment, please.' He got to his feet. 'Bacci!'

'I'm sorry, I didn't know—'

'Pick up the phone! Ask him if he hired a car last time he was in Florence!' He'd had to break off for lack of an English verb that he remembered as soon as Bacci pronounced it.

'I did.'

'And you drove around sightseeing? Out of Florence?'

'A couple of times, yes.'

'Did you see anything you liked?'

Bacci's translation met with silence.

'Mr Maxwell, there's no law in this country against your buying a piece of property, and if you were intending to remove money from your own country without paying tax on it, that's not of prime importance now. I'm hoping to save your daughter's life.'

'It was a present for Debbie. She likes it here but that place she's got is no more than a hole in the wall. She's used to space back home.'

'And to riding.'

'That's right. It was partly my wife's idea. She felt we should get her a healthier place, one where we could stay with her when we come over here.'

'Your daughter had no intention of returning to America?'

'She said not.'

'Did you quarrel about it?'

'I didn't say that. And I don't see what harm there is in buying a place for my daughter. The one I found was run down, anyway, and had been empty for years.'

'Not quite empty.'

'Sure it's empty. I dealt with the owner personally, and he hasn't set foot in the place since the war. Besides, I looked all of it over as soon as I saw it, persuaded the caretaker there to show us around.'

'Did you tell him you were interested in buying?'

'I did not. I hadn't decided then.'

'Did you tell your daughter?'

'No, I wanted to surprise her. It was Dorothy's idea. We were going to tell her on her birthday, that's two weeks from today.'

'Who does know?'

'The Count himself, the owner, that is, and his local agent. I had the Count send him my plans for the work I wanted to do on the buildings. If they weren't acceptable to the local council I wasn't going to buy.'

'If you submitted plans to the local council a great many people must know about them.'

'Listen, this has got nothing to do with what happened to Debbie. Whoever knows about those plans doesn't know they're mine. My name wasn't mentioned at all.'

'Were the plans approved?'

'They were.'

'You knew that two people had contracts with the owner?'

'I know one person has. The other only buys the grass each summer and has no rights at all over the land. He's allowed to cultivate a certain amount as a favour.'

'And the other?'

'That's this caretaker I mentioned. A good lawyer could have dealt with that. The Count advised me to put the house in my daughter's own name. Her rental contract runs out shortly and she can say she's homeless. If it didn't come off, the worst thing that could have happened is that it would have taken a few years to move him out.'

'You haven't signed the sales contract?'

'No.'

'Do you still intend to buy?'

'I most certainly do not!'

'I see. I think we may well find your daughter now.'

'Now listen, I've been in business all my life and I know who I can trust. Nobody knows I was buying that place except the owner!'

'Who introduced you to him?'

'A friend of mine from New York.'

'Did you tell him why you wanted the introduction?'

'No, I did not. He does a lot of business in Turin and I just told him I was going there.'

'I take it he's not a close friend, in that case?'

'There are friends you like and friends you don't like.'

'How did you know he knew the owner?'

'Through a mutual friend at the Consulate.'

'Who told you who owned the villa?'

'The caretaker who showed us the place—and he doesn't know my name either.'

It came back to the same thing. The only person who could have let it out was the girl herself.

'Mr Maxwell, remembering that your daughter's life is at stake, do you swear to me that she didn't know about this?'

'I swear she didn't know.'

And it was plain that he wasn't lying. Only as an apparent afterthought did the Captain ask:

'Were you intending to sign the contract on this trip?'

'I was.'

'So you already had a flight booked when you heard what had happened?'

'Luckily, yes—Listen, any information I've given you is in confidence, remember that. You can't use my daughter to take advantage of me.'

'Bacci, tell him not to leave the hotel.' He hung up.

The Brigadier knocked and came in. 'It's Scano's boy. He's left the villa. He had a moped hidden in some bushes not far away and now he's turned on to the track going up the mountain. My man wants to know what to do; if he follows him up there he'll be seen . . .'

'Tell him to come back, we can't take risks—and bring me a glass of water, will you?'

A little later, when he was along, the Captain dialled Guarnaccia's number at Pitti.

'The Marshal's not back yet.'

'When do you expect him?'

'I expected him over an hour ago.'

'He hasn't telephoned?'

'No. It's not like him, especially as we haven't eaten. I don't want to send anybody off to the mensa in case something's happened and he needs us. Should I ask him to ring you when he comes in?'

'I have to go out . . .' What had Guarnaccia to do that was more important than this case? This was no time to disappear.

'Are you still there, sir? He's coming in now . . .'

There was a cough and a deep breath before the Marshal said: 'Guarnaccia.'

'I've been trying to reach you.'

'Yes, Lorenzini said so.'

'I thought I'd better keep you up to date—you left here in such a rush, you didn't say whether you had any thoughts on the villa business . . .'

'No, no . . . I haven't had chance.'

'Maxwell was intending to buy the villa.'

'I see.'

'And to get rid of the gamekeeper.'

'I see.'

'Obviously, that means he's involved.'

'As base-man?'

'Probably.'

'I see.'

'Is something the matter?'

'No . . .'

'Your Brigadier was worried when you didn't come in.'

'There was an attempted suicide at the prison. I waited.'

'Cipolla?'

'Yes. I don't think I can be much help to you, to be honest. I don't know the people. If you were to ask the Brigadier . . . I've never even seen this man Pratesi.'

'Pratesi?'

'The sausage factory we passed, just before the village. I thought the Brigadier had told you he suspected him of running some racket on the side.'

'He did. You think it might be drugs?'

'Drugs? No, it never occurred to me—but then I didn't ask him, I just assumed it was meat. It might be drugs, of course.'

'It's probable that the kidnapped girl was an addict.'

'In that case . . .'

'There must have been some point of contact. It's not a professional job.'

'I see what you mean. It's just that I haven't had time to think about it and I only thought that with all those shepherds in the area there was bound to be some traffic in illegally slaughtered lamb. The Brigadier would be the person to ask—you're still out there?'

'Yes. I'll talk to him.'

'If there's nothing else . . .' the Marshal said anxiously. 'I've got to go next door . . . Cipolla's sister . . . I'm sorry I'm not more help.'

'That's right,' said the Brigadier distractedly, 'lamb . . . I think I can smell something burning . . .'

'You'll have to leave them to it. I want you to get in touch with the Mayor and tell him I need to have the Council offices opened up. Then get hold of the alderman in charge of planning and apologize if we're disturbing his supper but we'll need him. And the Substitute had better be with me—tell Bacci he can take my car down to

Florence, I don't really need him and the Substitute can take me back with him . . . He surely won't come out this far in a taxi . . .'

He had to try three of the numbers which the Substitute had given him on identical slips of paper, each of which had "after eight-thirty" written in small, neat writing across the bottom.

The first two numbers were restaurants. The third one wasn't.

'I'll come immediately.' He rang off before the Captain could ask him whether he would drive up.

It was a little after ten o'clock by the time the three men gathered in the council chamber over the post office and unrolled the plans on the long oak table. The young architect, who served part-time as alderman in charge of town planning, had indeed been interrupted at his supper, accepted a cigar and a light from the Substitute before beginning to explain. He had to talk above the noise of the discothèque music coming from the Communist club next door.

'Here's where the road to Taverna passes behind the villa—there's a bridle path leading from there to the stables, this double dotted line here. This is the main driveway up here, opening on what used to be a road down to Florence.'

'Can you still get all the way down to Florence on it?'

'If the weather's dry and if you don't mind how you treat your car—or maybe you could only do it in a jeep, I've never tried it. Most people only use that road to get to the villa itself and the two farms beyond it. It's in reasonable repair up to that point, but then it forks, one fork joining the Taverna road again, a short stretch that's in good shape, and the other going down to the city. That hasn't been touched for over fifteen years.'

'Go on.'

'These are the stables, separate from the house itself.

This half and all the top floor are to be converted into a self-contained cottage for guests. The rest of the ground floor is to be garage space for two cars. The stone barn over here is to have stabling for two horses, a harness room and a hayloft above. Along here there's a high wall—dividing the present stables and the paddock from the lawns and villa—with a small wooden door in it. Part of the wall, as you can see, is to be knocked down to allow the drive to pass through to the garages. There are no structural changes in the villa itself except that the wall between it and the gamekeeper's quarters is to be demolished to make a bigger kitchen. There are two new bathrooms.'

'What's this line?' asked the Substitute. 'A new boundary?'

'Yes. That's where the land to be sold with the villa finishes, the gardens and paddock and this one meadow. As for the rest—I don't know what he intends, but it's agricultural land and has to be sold or rented as such.'

'Did you know who the prospective owner was,' asked the Captain, 'when you discussed these plans?'

'No, they were sent from Turin via the agent in the village here. I know the agent well and I'm sure he didn't know either.'

'He would have told you?'

'Of course.'

'There weren't even any rumours about who it might be?'

'At first there were. Everyone thought Pratesi was the buyer because he's been talking for years about building a bigger place, rearing his own pigs and growing his own feed. But once the contents of these plans got around the rumours died down and people began to say that the family must be coming back.'

'Would Pratesi have had that sort of money?'

'Who knows? The agent's estimates are here if you

want to look at them.'

'I'll need to take them with me.'

'He's made a packet from that factory, there's no doubt about that. It's high quality stuff and his salami and his wild boar sausages are known all over Tuscany. And then he's always got some racket or other going on the side—more than one, I should think. The Brigadier's always out to catch him at it. They're deadly enemies, those two. They've even been known to have words in the piazza.'

'But Pratesi never submitted plans to you?'

'No. Even so, I'm sure he's serious. If the family does come back he'll be furious. His land adjoins theirs for one thing, and more importantly, it's the only way he can expand in this area to include substantial buildings.'

'Would you have given him planning permission?'

'I think we would. He's a pretty odious character but he provides work. With so many people leaving the land, something has to hold the village together. As it is, the majority of people go down to Florence to work. He'd have got permission all right.'

'Does he have much to do with the gamekeeper at the villa?'

'I rather think the gamekeeper does a bit of illegal slaughtering for him, and they often go down to Florence together at night, gambling I think.'

'Then that's all we need to know.'

At eleven-fifteen they shook hands with the architect out in the piazza. Apart from the lamps that gave a yellow glow to the leaves, the only light came from the big windows of the Communist club which was packed on both floors, its discothèque going full swing.

Once he got started, the Brigadier didn't draw breath for more than half an hour.

'But I'll catch him at it yet,' he wound up, wagging a threatening hand at the window. 'And I've told him so!'

The Captain had to interrupt him; 'You know he's involved with the guard at the villa? It means that they're probably in this together and that if Scano's boy risked going to the villa something must have gone badly wrong. This may not be a professional job but Scano's boy isn't that much of an amateur. What went wrong was presumably the death of Piladu's son. There's still a missing link but I think we'll find it in Florence, not up here. In any case, we can't wait. If something's gone wrong, then we have to try and get the girl out while she's still alive, if she is alive. If Maxwell pays the ransom I don't think there's much hope. At the moment he's under control, but I don't want to give him time to try going over my head.' He said this without looking at the Substitute, though he would have liked to see his reaction.

'But we can't go up there at night!' complained the Brigadier. 'It'd be a fiasco. You know they sleep with both eyes open and a rifle under the pillow—not to mention the fact that it's still lambing season and most of them will be up all night! I don't want my lads shot at in the dark and yours don't know the ground.'

'I'm going up there in the daytime,' the Captain said. 'And all I need is to have you go with me and the warrants. The helicopter boys will see to the rest. You know as well as I do that Rudolfo's the only one involved who has a house up there. There's nowhere else the girl can be.'

'Poor Rudolfo,' said the Substitute, watching the other two curiously. 'I wonder what they promised him?'

'Very little, I imagine,' said the Captain irritably, 'and he wouldn't have got it, either, but he was going to lose his grazing rights, which for him meant he was going to lose everything.'

'He still is,' the Brigadier said. 'He still is, the young idiot, and just as he was getting on his feet. Sometimes I don't know if I wouldn't rather be . . . I don't know. I think I ought to check on my motor-bike patrol.'

In the taxi that had waited all evening in the piazza for them, the Captain glanced sideways at the point of glowing ash and said politely, 'I hope I didn't take you away from something more important this evening.'

'As a matter of fact you did,' replied the Substitute gravely, 'but for heaven's sake don't worry about it, you've got enough to worry about already.'

It was impossible to see in the dark whether the habitual spark of irony accompanied this remark.

The Captain took this problem, along with all his others and his irritation, to bed with him.

CHAPTER 10

At ten-thirty next morning Captain Maestrangelo stood at the window in his office looking down intently at the street. A packet of aspirin and half a glass of water stood on the tray on his desk. He had slept badly and woken badly and was fighting against the sort of headache that usually came on after a big case was finished. It was a devastating headache but, oddly enough, as a rule he didn't mind it. He would suffer it, even nurse it along, for a couple of days, and when it went he would forget the case along with the pain. But if it came on now . . .

His face was pale and his eyes half closed against the sunlight. Nevertheless he stayed there watching. There was hardly any traffic, just a few parked cars and a cluster of mopeds around the door of the bar opposite. People were coming out from Palm Sunday Mass at the church of Ognissanti, pausing to chat to families going in to the last service and then passing under his window carrying sprays of olive leaves. Most of them went into the newsagent's and the bar to buy the Sunday edition of the

Nazione and a tray of cakes wrapped with gold and white paper and curly gold ribbons.

If she didn't come by twelve they would have to leave anyway. He was taking a group of his own men plus dogs and their handlers out to the helicopter base where he could brief them together with the pilots. It wasn't an easy operation and the timing of it was important. Sunday was the one day on which most of the mountain shepherds ate their midday meal indoors. Their wives and children joined them on Saturday night and on Sunday they ate together before the visitors went down the mountain in a long procession.

It was then that Rudolfo, if he wanted to avoid suspicion, would lead his flock down to the villa.

The Captain intended to make his attack at one-thirty when the fewest possible people would be out in the open. He couldn't leave Florence any later than twelve o'clock. There was no sign of her in the street but a taxi might draw up at any moment. If they had given his note to her exactly as he had said . . . Even then she might have decided not to answer him, or she could have let it be seen by accident before knowing what it was.

There were few people left in the street. The occasional car went by but no taxis. Then he saw her. She was coming along the opposite pavement on foot and was looking up at the buildings as if she were not sure of being in the right street. She paused a moment, looking worriedly across at the main entrance, and then she crossed the road. The Captain picked up his telephone before it had time to ring.

'Bring her up.'

It was ten to eleven. He hoped she had made up her mind to talk and would not make him lose valuable time persuading her.

'Signora.' He opened the door for her himself and dismissed the escort with a nod.

'My husband doesn't know I'm here.'

'Please sit down.'

'I don't want to waste your time. I told Debbie about the house only John didn't know. You don't know my husband, Captain,—he's not like this; he's an impatient man and used to having his own way, but he isn't like this.'

'I understand.'

'Yes . . . of course you understand. You must be so used to always seeing people under stress . . . I told Debbie about the house because they'd quarrelled, she and her father, and I was afraid that if she didn't try and make it up with him he would change his mind. They're very alike and both of them are stubborn. Debbie had said she didn't want to come back to the States. She never would say why but I felt almost sure she was doing it against him, either to spite him or to gain his attention. She may have had other reasons. I think my husband told you on the phone that buying the house over here was my idea. I thought that way I could bring them together. I have no children of my own and I really thought I could be a mother to Debbie . . . If I tell you that was one of the main reasons why I married John . . . But I just couldn't reach her. It's a terrible thing to see someone unhappy when you want to help them and you can't. We saw so little of each other, and I suppose it was too late. She was almost grown up and there was no reason why she should want me. She didn't choose me, I've often told myself that. I thought maybe I was just being selfish, it's so difficult to analyse your emotions. After a while I decided it was best to try and help her get on better with her father, and now by interfering between them I've been the cause of her being kidnapped. If I'd known how important it was about the house—I didn't understand until I got your note. I heard John's side of your conversation but he wouldn't talk about it afterwards. He said he wanted to call the Ambassador.'

'Did he call?' asked the Captain quickly.

'He did. But as far as I could make out the Ambassador was away. He has to call him again this morning. That's why I was able to get out alone. I said I needed some air, but if I don't go back soon . . . Do you think you'll find Debbie?'

'I'll find her.'

'When I think about her . . . She never liked the dark. I keep thinking she's in the dark, I don't know why that should be. They wouldn't keep her in the dark?'

The Captain frowned and murmured something sufficiently incomprehensible for her to take it as a negative.

'You must think I'm a very foolish woman, Captain.'

'I think you are a very good woman, Mrs Maxwell,' he said, rising.

'I'm sure I don't understand why.'

'It would need my Sub-lieutenant', he said, ringing for the escort, 'to explain.'

Bacci wasn't sure if he'd done the right thing. He should have asked the Captain but with the Substitute's eyes fixed on him he hadn't felt able to, and later there had never been time. Well, in theory he was doing what he was supposed to do since this was the time of day he always spent with Katrine and he had been told not to vary the routine. It would have been different if the other girls had been in the flat, but they were both away for the weekend. He had reasoned that, even if they couldn't talk there, the morning concert might do her some good, that she had never willingly set foot out of the flat since it happened, that in any case he had a father's responsibility towards his younger sister, and he had promised to go and hear her. So it had seemed better all round that they should go. If they had stayed in the flat . . .

The sunshine was pouring in through a high window

on the right, warming a square of the dark red polished floor and making the rest of the room look gloomy by comparison. All the seats were filled and a number of people were standing by the door. The audience consisted chiefly of parents of the conservatory students.

The pianist was complaining about the sunbeam which was falling across her face so that she couldn't see her music. Someone got a long pole and closed the shutter.

Bacci didn't follow a note of the "Primavera" sonata. The violinist was a heavy, dark-skinned girl from South America, and both the girls had graduated from the Florence conservatory the previous year, according to the programme notes . . .

The music flowed around him but without soothing his nerves. They couldn't, after all, have stayed in the flat. He could just see the top of his mother's head, right at the front . . . There was no reason why the Captain should ever find out. He didn't ask what they did or said every morning, but left it to Bacci to report any snippet of information he managed to get from her. Sometimes he was so tense in her presence that he couldn't speak at all. If he could have talked to her in Italian it would have been different, but his correct English, which he had learned from his mother who had had an English governess, and which he only ever spoke with her friends or on a case that required it, was of no use to him now. They talked to each other exchanging facts but not communicating.

Her fair hair was so long that it touched his hand whenever they sat side by side. He absently slid his programme nearer to her so that it touched him now, glancing at her out of the corner of his eye. She was very pale. He couldn't remember her being as pale as that since she left the hospital. She didn't seem to be concentrating on the performance because her eyes kept moving from side to side, although she sat very still.

After a while they clapped, and then his sister walked

on to the low platform that was surrounded by a frothy sea of pink and white azalea plants. She had put her hair up so as to look older than her sixteen years but even so she straightened her music and her shoulders with such self-consciousness that the maturity of her voice came as a shock to him just as it always did. Had Katrine too been surprised? She was frowning a little as if trying to concentrate, and she was even paler than before.

'Are you all right?' he whispered, leaning closer.

'Yes . . .' She took the programme from his hand as if wanting to know what the song was, but her eyes were shut as she bent her head over it. He pointed to '*Pergolesi*' and she lifted her head again to look from side to side.

If she really hadn't felt up to coming out she would surely have said? She had seemed quite tranquil as they walked in the sunshine through the crowded cathedral square where spectator stands were being erected ready for the Easter celebrations. He had explained to her about the imitation dove that would fly out from the high altar during the Easter mass and light a great cart of fireworks. He had promised to take her to see it. If she really hadn't wanted to come out . . . The trouble was that she would never say, she would only look away and murmur vaguely, 'You decide . . .'

It was difficult to know whether she had understood everything he had tried to explain to her about his being involved in a case in which she was the chief witness, about his career, and how he had a mother and sister to support.

'We have to wait.'

'It doesn't matter.'

It mattered to him. Sometimes the Captain caught him staring at him fixedly, willing him to get the case under Instruction. He couldn't hold out much longer if only because he wasn't getting any sleep. Sooner or later he would be too exhausted to think straight and would give up the fight against himself. Would she say the same thing afterwards? 'It doesn't matter . . .' But she had to cope with a foreign language too. Some days were better; she would curl up on the sofa and talk dreamily about their taking a trip to Norway together. She barely seemed to notice if he stroked her hair as they talked, but if he moved she would say quickly, 'Don't go away,' and bring his hand back to her forehead. Then he would be filled with tenderness.

She was staring at the platform again. She wouldn't understand the archaic Italian of the song, and he slipped a pencil from his pocket to scribble a translation on the programme for her.

'If you love me, if you breathe
Only for me, sweet shepherd boy . . .'

The irony, he thought, was lost in the translation but he went on with it anyway. He was desperate for her to learn Italian. How could he make love to her in English? He had to touch her arm to make her look at the programme.

'But if you think I have to
Love you in return . . .'

Her gaze was wandering, he knew, but he finished the verse.

'Little shepherd, you're an easy one to fool.'

She had looked at the first lines but now she wasn't reading any of it. He followed her eyes to the sides of the room where there were huge tapestries depicting nymphs and shepherds playing in a landscape filled with trees and winding streams. The greens and golds were all faded and darkened to a dull blackish colour that looked all the drabber in the presence of so many fresh flowers. The song was almost over.

*'Se tu m'ami, se tu sospiri
Sol per me, gentil pastor . . .'*

He moved as soon as he saw the first bead of sweat

break on her pallid face, and then he was almost too late.

'Get me outside.'

People were clapping as he stumbled between the rows of seats with her and out into the garden, where she reached out one hand to clutch at the trunk of a flowering cherry, then doubled up over his arm to vomit into a tidy bed of daffodils.

Men in forage caps were milling around below in the courtyard, their voices and footsteps resounding throughout the building. They were ready to leave. In the Captain's office the Substitute snapped his briefcase shut and his registrar handed over the warrants that had been made out for Rudolfo, Scano's boy and the gamekeeper.

'And the other two?' the Substitute asked.

'Pratesi I'll have brought in but not arrested yet. I don't think he'll give us much trouble once he's confronted with the others. He won't know them, of course, apart from the base-man, nor they him, but it will have its effects all the same. Demontis, the much despised brother-in-law, I had hoped to get by now. The man who's watching him followed him as near as possible to the mountain the first time but he couldn't go any further without being seen—the same problem we had with Scano's boy yesterday. Since then he's been waiting for him higher up on various tracks. Once he hits on the right track he should be able to follow him to the place where he leaves the food and then watch who picks it up. It's a job that takes time. He'll get there in the end but we can't wait. There might be some news this morning since he usually goes up on Sunday—though this week he's been twice . . .'

'Which means?'

'That they've lost a feeder. It might well have been Piladu's son. But I still don't know why Scano's boy risked going to the villa unless they've lost a guard, too, which would really put them in difficulty. There must be one other guard besides him and Rudolfo, who's always there but who has to milk and make his cheese and who—'

He was interrupted by the telephone.

'Yes? Speak up, would you? There's a lot of noise coming from outside. Wait . . .' He took up a pen and began to write quickly. 'That's all right, you needn't explain exactly where, the Brigadier will tell me . . . No, you needn't do anything except come back in and write your report. We're going up there now.' He slipped the note into his pocket.

'You can give me that warrant for Demontis. We're ready to go.'

But the phone rang again.

'Sub-lieutenant Bacci on his way up with Miss Nilsen. It's urgent.'

The Captain looked at his watch.

'I've got ten minutes . . .'

'Do you want me to see them?'

'There may be something I need to know. I'll see them next door if you would prepare that warrant for me?'

'Of course.' The Substitute signed to his registrar to sit down again.

'If we can pick them all up at the same time we won't lose any of them.'

When he saw the state the girl was in he sat her in an armchair and sent his adjutant to get her something to drink.

'A brandy might be best . . . and a glass of water.'

'She insisted on coming straight here,' said Bacci, who was almost as pale as she was.

'In ten minutes I have to leave. Has she already talked to you?'

'In the taxi coming here.'

'Then you tell me everything in brief, and quickly. If

you know who the contact was, then tell me that first.'

'There were any number of possibilities, though one in particular is most likely.'

'What do you mean by any number?'

'Miss Maxwell was perfectly normal in her behaviour at school—except that she was perhaps too much the model student—but every so often she would disappear, usually for about three days, once for a whole week. Nobody remarked on it because all the students are foreign and occasionally take trips home or go on sightseeing tours. A lot of them are studying other things besides Italian and so they take time off to prepare for exams. Nevertheless, when she disappeared for a week without saying anything to Katrine who was her closest friend, Katrine went round to the flat a number of times, thinking she must be ill. The third time she went she got Debbie to come to the door but not to let her in. She had to try another three times over two days before she succeeded in talking her way in. Twice there was a man in the background but not the same one each time, she's sure. She was obviously very unhappy and managed to conceal it most of the time.'

'What was she taking?'

'Cocaine.'

'Then it's easy to see where her money went . . .'

'Yes. When Katrine eventually got in she found her friend in a state of physical and mental collapse. But within two days she was back at school and behaving as if nothing had happened.'

'Where did she get the stuff?'

'The usual bar. She told Katrine everything but nobody else knew. It seems she dressed herself up in the most provocative way possible when she got into this state and behaved like a caricature of the rich foreigner. Out of some sort of desperation she seemed to want to degrade herself. She usually left with one of the men. Afterwards she would be full of remorse and would return to playing the clean-living model student. Katrine wanted to help her. That was why once or twice Debbie let her cash the money order for her. Then Katrine would look after the money for the month, but it didn't work. Debbie disappeared just the same and then rang to ask for the money. Katrine was afraid of what might happen if she didn't pay up.'

'Did she ever go with her to the bar?'

'Once, having failed to dissuade her from going. That's one of the main reasons why she's been so frightened. She knew that some of the men there were shepherds who came in from the country and that all this must be connected with the kidnapping. She hadn't recognised any of the people or even seen their faces but the thought that they must know her was enough.'

They glanced across at her. She was watching them over the rim of the glass, looking from one to the other of their faces, trying to follow their too rapid talk.

'And this is why she stayed the night with her?'

'Yes. The pattern was predictable. It always happened when her allowance arrived. The pushers knew exactly when to expect her and if she didn't turn up they would telephone her. There was one man in particular, as I said; he seemed to have her under his control.'

'Does she know his name?'

'No. She doesn't know any of their names, but she remembers that he had a long scar running right up his hand. It looked recent.'

'Who was selling her the stuff, this same man?'

'He was controlling her supply but it all came from someone else. Katrine never saw the pusher but they referred to him as "Baffetti". I suppose he had a moustache.'

'Garau . . .'

'You know him?'

'Only too well . . . He's inside for having slit a man's throat. I wonder . . . Just a moment.'

He made a quick call to the hospital next door. When he got the staff nurse of the ward he wanted she said:

'I can tell you without going to look. The scar goes right up to his elbow and he got it in a fight just like the scar he's going to have round his throat.'

'He's going to be all right, then?'

'Only because he was lucky.'

Garau too had been lucky, to be charged with grievous bodily harm instead of murder. Maybe the scarred man had suspected something and wanted a cut of the ransom. It must have been he who telephoned the flat. The Captain didn't even know his name since the fight had happened in another part of the city and he had only read about it in the papers. Now Garau would be charged with kidnapping. The Captain had been right about their having lost a guard as well as a feeder. Garau was the missing link who sold drugs to both Debbie Maxwell and to the shepherds. And then he had jeopardized the whole job by landing himself inside. That was why Scano's boy had risked going back to the base-man. Had they found another guard? Somebody must be up there to take over when Rudolfo came down . . .

'The girl's allowance must have just arrived when this happened,' the Captain said. 'Somebody tried to phone her at the flat. We found hardly any money. Where is it?'

'Katrine has it in her account.' Each time she heard her name the girl stared at them more anxiously than ever, as if she wanted to speak, to excuse herself, but was too exhausted. 'They paid it in the day before. Debbie was determined that this time she would fight it off. There wasn't room for her to stay in the flat with the three other girls so they decided that Katrine should stay in Piazza Pitti in Debbie's flat. They turned the telephone down and spent most of the evening at the cinema. Both of them were frightened before this even happened.'

'Did she say anything more about the messages for Maxwell?'

'That she should have given him the letter a week after his arrival. They knew he would be at the Excelsior.'

'Did she know that Maxwell was buying a house here?'

'I don't know. She didn't say so.'

'Leave it for now . . .' The Captain went over to the girl and asked her gently in English: 'Are you feeling better?'

She didn't answer him but said: 'Her father's so rich. I thought he would just pay up and then take her home. It was the only way to put an end to it—I even thought it might help her.'

'Perhaps it will.' The Captain was thinking of her note.

'They might have killed me, mightn't they? They might have killed me, that's what I couldn't stop thinking about. I don't think I've thought about anything else since it happened. I thought they were afraid of me too.'

'Don't worry. It will soon be over now.'

'You will find Debbie?'

'I'll find her.'

'I want to telephone my father. I want to go home to Norway.'

He had her driven back to her flat and sent a guard with her. There was no reason why, once they had taken her statement, she shouldn't go home to Norway until the case came to trial. That could easily be in over a year's time.

She left the room without a backward glance.

'Bacci, come with me. You did a good job on that, now let's see you in action.'

'Maestrangelo!' They were in the corridor and the Substitute was coming towards them, but the Captain had caught a glimpse of the figure that turned to go down the stairs beyond him. It was the Prefect, and that could only mean one thing. In theory he had been prepared for it all along, but that it should happen now, right now . . .

'Maestrangelo.' The Substitute reached them. He had his briefcase in one hand, a cigar and a sheet of paper in the other. 'The Prefect has had a call from the Minister. The American Ambassador has been in touch with him.'

'I see.'

'They want the inquiry suspended for twenty-four hours. You'll know better than I do what that means.'

'That he's already got the ransom money here, that it was probably on its way already as payment for the house. And if they only want twenty-four hours then they've already made the appointment to hand it over. Did they say so?'

'No. They weren't saying anything.'

'If they pay up she'll be killed. From what the Nilsen girl has just told me Garau is our missing link, and with him in prison they're in too tight a corner. If she's released and lets out the story about "Baffetti" pushing cocaine. There's also the boyfriend with the scar who's a threat. He's still in hospital with a slit throat but he can talk and might know something. The job's so messed up . . . it's messy, it's amateur and it's personal. Unless I get to her before they pay up we might as well give up looking.'

'You weren't able to convince Maxwell?'

'I could only convince his wife, whose one concern is to save her stepdaughter. Maxwell still thinks he can run this himself, pay up and leave with his daughter rather than keep his money and have the case come to court so that his affairs might have to be examined—that could cost him more than the ransom. If he doesn't believe me it's because he doesn't want to, and if I save his daughter's life it will be in spite of him.'

There was nothing else the Captain could say. If he couldn't move now, then the girl's death would not be his responsibility, and frustration was something he had learned to live with. But his headache was worse and it was seven minutes past twelve. He had everything he needed to arrest the whole gang. The noise down in the courtyard was getting louder as the men began to wonder why they weren't leaving. He looked at the Substitute who stuck the cigar between his teeth and handed him the sheet of paper,saying:

'Thank you. Have to tell them something, you see. Make a good impression. That's the warrant for the Demontis brother. You'll ring me when you get back? Wait . . . at this number. I'm already late and so are you—eight minutes late. Good luck.'

CHAPTER 11

Only by flying over it was it possible to see that what everyone called "the mountain", and what from below seemed to be a sudden flinty eruption among the smoothly-combed Tuscan hills, was really a plateau, a long arm sweeping west from the Appenines, disconnected from the backbone of mountains by the valley of the river Arno. Most of the plateau, with the exception of the topmost ridge and some patches of rock-strewn pasture, was covered by miles of thick, gloomy woodland. Bacci gazed down at the giant shadows passing across it as the wind drove huge clouds about the sky. It was cold in the helicopter and the mountain below looked as bleak and hostile as it always did, no matter what the weather. The Brigadier was expounding something or other to the Captain, beating time with his big, open hand and repeating himself interminably. Bacci had only spoken once during the journey, asking the Captain:

'Why did they let Katrine go?'

'Rudolfo would have backed out if they'd killed her. They needed their scapegoat. Now he can't, it's too late, whatever they do.'

The Captain had explained patiently, but his face was pale and annoyed-looking. Perhaps he had guessed something, but if he had he wouldn't say anything until the case was over. For Bacci it was over already. She had walked out without even saying goodbye, without so much as a glance at him. The pilot was talking into his radio and looking across at another helicopter which then dropped back out of sight. The pilots seemed to be worrying about the weather, either because it was so changeable or because of the wind, he wasn't sure which. He heard one of them say:

'This cloud'll come down on us if the wind drops.'

'We'll be away by then . . .'

They weren't going to land. It wasn't possible. Suddenly they had turned and were sweeping back in a wide circle. The Captain and the Brigadier were looking down intently at a white patch moving slowly down the lower slopes of the mountain. Bacci stared down without understanding what they were surprised about. A shepherd moving down with his sheep.

'Wait,' the Brigadier was saying. 'Come in lower . . . I thought as much. It's not Rudolfo, it's his young brother. But why . . .?'

'If they're short of guards,' the Captain said, 'perhaps Rudolfo will be forced to stay up there. I don't see how else they can manage.'

'Neither can that little lad manage . . . milking and cheesemaking on his own . . . Something's not as it should be.'

'It's as well he's out of the way. We don't want anybody unnecessarily hurt.'

'That's true . . .' But the Brigadier continued to murmur to himself as they turned and took up their course again. The pilot was still talking into his radio. Bacci was finding it more and more difficult to keep in contact with what was going on around him, probably because of lack of sleep. He might have been watching everything through a thick glass partition, their voices seemed so far away. She had walked out without looking at him, as if nothing . . .

He saw the faint mark of a footpath below, and then they were flying over a scattering of grey houses with ramshackle red-tiled roofs, the low walls around them broken down and grassy. Rusted farm implements stuck out of the ground here and there. Some of the houses were half gutted by bombs or fire, but all the ones that had some sort of roof had smoke rising slowly from the chimneys. Sheep stood among the rubble and grass, huddled together against the cold wind. The Brigadier, who had been talking about partisans, began pointing and giving directions to the pilot, who relayed them to the helicopters behind. They flew over a lone farmhouse that had no smoke coming from it, and then they were rising and turning in a sickeningly tight circle. One by one the rest of the helicopters were dipping and slowing near the house, spilling their burden of green-clad men and leaping dogs without stopping, then whirring away to make the same tight circle. The Captain was talking into his radio below the noise of the rotor-blades, and the figures below had surrounded the house and moved in. Then they were spreading out again in a widening halo, looking up. They and the landscape began to spin slowly and loom closer as the Captain said, 'We're coming down.'

All Bacci could think of was that he didn't want to step out on to that cold, wind-whipped mountain and have this whole scene become real. But they were moving already and he was clinging to a rope-ladder that dangled above the rocky ground, with the wind whipping his head. When the hard, stony earth crashed up against his feet causing him to stumble sideways, he began to come to his senses, pulling in a sharp breath of cold air. The Captain overtook him and was running towards the dilapidated house where the only door was crashing repeatedly open and shut in the wind, shedding its peeling scraps of paint.

The room had no window. It must have once housed beasts. It was so dark inside that Bacci couldn't see anything at first, though he was aware of the room being full of people talking quietly and of the hot breath of the overexcited dogs. It was only gradually that the whites of the dogs' eyes became visible, then the paleness of the mens' faces. Last of all he made out the darker shape of the Captain at the far side of the room. Bacci pushed between the others to join him where he stood looking down at a mattress soaked through with blood and a thick chain dangling from the low metal bedstead.

When the Captain turned he seemed to look right through his Sub-lieutenant. His eyes were narrower and his face more strained than Bacci could ever remember.

'Brigadier,' the Captain said, and the Brigadier appeared in the gloom, a little out of breath. The Captain turned back to the bed and they looked at it together.

'Dear God . . .'

'Leave that door open!' the Captain ordered without looking round. 'We need the light!'

'Nobody could have lived through this,' the Brigadier said, 'Nobody . . . It's everywhere. Look at the walls even. Rudolfo couldn't have done it. Of course there'd be somebody else with him, like you said . . . of course there would. Because he couldn't have done this. Dear God . . . What do we do now?'

The Captain had taken a twig from near the dead wood fire in the makeshift fireplace and was lifting something stringy out of the mess. It could have been grass or even small plants. It was impossible to tell. He let them drop back carefully. There was a flat, greyish pillow on the bed. It was twisted and most of it was covered thickly with dark blood. A soaked exercise book lay underneath it. He tried to lift the pages open with the twig but they wouldn't separate. It was a job for the technicians. He straightened and stood back. Signalling the Brigadier and Bacci to get out of the way, he said:

'Let the dogs through.'

'Do you think there's much chance of finding the body?' one of the handlers asked him as the dogs sniffed around the bed, whining softly.

'There's a possibility. They're panicked enough to have made a mess of this, too.'

The dogs were taken outside.

You will find her?

I'll find her . . .

The Captain began pacing up and down the small room as though he were a prisoner there.

'Don't move! Any of you!'

The scene was almost identical in each house; the smoky gloom as they entered, the dark red glow of the wood fire where a basting stick of rosemary lay in a tray of liquid lamb's fat. Round the table, six or seven pairs of eyes glinting in the dark as the men moved in, one on guard with a machine-gun while the others searched. A cheese room, the best and airiest with a window, upstairs a big airless bedroom with nothing in it but a narrow bed and some old blankets, down to the dark room again with the bread and roast lamb lying half-eaten on the oilcloth-covered table, and their questions which met with an almost palpable silence. One house was empty, the hearth heaped with cold grey ash and charred logs, one chair standing beside it. On the table a round yellow cheese, a dirty straw wine flask, half a raw ham and some broken sheets of dark, unleavened bread. The shepherd had been nowhere in sight when they neared the house but he appeared while they were searching it to stand leaning his chin on his crook and watch them with narrow, dispassionate eyes as though the house were nothing to do with him. Still watching them, he took some food from the table, stood and ate some of it, put the rest in his pockets and walked slowly out.

In another house an enormously fat woman with a long pigtail had just put a batch of little yellow Palm Sunday cakes on the table.

It was the group that came out of there that saw the dogs running and pawing around a patch of scrub near a rocky hollow.

Inside Rudolfo's house the Captain was still pacing to and fro while Bacci and the Brigadier watched him in silence.

'He can't have paid. It's only an hour since they asked for a twenty-four-hour suspension. An hour ago! I don't believe he's paid! Why should they do it? Why? Nobody knew we were coming up here. Nobody.'

The other two stood still, watching him. The room had two chairs in it, one of formica and rust-pitted metal, the other of wood and straw. There wasn't even a real table, only an old door propped over a manger. Half a flask of wine stood on it with some cheese rinds and scraps of bread, fresh bread brought up from the city.

Two men with dogs appeared in the hard light of the doorway. The Captain stopped pacing.

'Well?'

'We haven't found her yet, but we've found something . . .'

He didn't stop to ask what but followed them out into the wind. The dogs had uncovered what they had found. Two men held back the bushes with thick-gloved hands to let the Captain through. The body was face down and there were a number of stab wounds in the back.

'Do you know who he is, sir?'

'Yes.' The Captain looked at the high-laced hunter's boots and the olive-green serge clothing. 'I don't know him but I know who he is. Turn him over, will you?'

One of the Brigadier's boys who was part of the group that came out of the nearest house came forward to look and exclaimed:

'But that's the gamekeeper from the villa!'

'Yes.'

'Who could have done that to his eyes?'

One eye was pushed right out of its socket.

The boy, a young National Service lad from the village, stepped back, the colour suddenly leaving his face. He ran off behind the bushes, clutching at his stomach.

The Captain climbed the side of the hollow, strode back to Rudolfo's house and sat down on one of the chairs, staring at the cold wood ash in the dark. The other two, who had been talking quietly when he came in, fell silent. The door was banging open and shut in the wind again. Bacci thought he should close it but the Captain had ordered that it be left open so he didn't move. Eventually the Brigadier found something to wedge it open. It was even colder in the room than outside, where at least the sun was quite strong when it came out.

The Captain was so tense in his chair that his head and back were buzzing with pain. The drone of the circling helicopters nagged at his nerves. He was wasting fuel and time. You can't surprise a mountain. He had said it himself. But he couldn't bring himself to go back down. When the helicopters were at their most distant it was possible to hear the moaning of the wind around the wooded slopes lower down the mountain, and the handlers calling orders to their dogs in German. The tenser his body became, the more loosely did his mind seem to ramble. He had done everything according to the rules, moved slowly and carefully, weighed every possibility, but the ground had slipped from under him. The

Substitute must have talked to the Prefect and the Minister by now, convincing them of Maestrangelo's reasons, his experience, his proven efficiency. What would he say now? It was ironic; the one time he had a Substitute who backed him up . . . And he hadn't the least idea how or why it had happened. That was surely ridiculous. Years of experience might count for nothing in a case of this kind if you were simply unlucky. But even then the possibilities didn't vary. Things went wrong but they were the things you knew might go wrong. If Maxwell hadn't paid . . .

Guarnaccia had said, "*I can't help you. I don't know the people.*" As if you could know all the people involved in every case you handled. It was true that if he had known more about them than just their criminal records he might have been able to work out why they had panicked and run, what might have happened, what they might have heard. "*Ask the Brigadier . . .*" The Brigadier at least knew the people, and so did his men . . .

"*That's the gamekeeper from the villa!*"

"*Who could have done that to his eyes?*"

A National Service recruit. A boy of eighteen or nineteen who probably couldn't cook spaghetti and who had run off to be sick at the sight of his first corpse.

'Who could have done that to his eyes?'

Practically a child. And his amazement was genuine. He didn't know.

The Captain let out a long breath.

'Brigadier?'

There was nobody there. He found them standing outside, the Brigadier expounding quietly but insistently, Bacci's eyes wandering over the bleak skyscape.

'Brigadier? Where could they hide that's not all that far away?'

'Nowhere except the other shepherds' houses.'

'Something empty.'

'Anything up here that has a roof on it is inhabited—how many of them do you think there are?'

'Two. And I want them alive. No shooting under any circumstances. Now tell me where they could hide. They're still up here, Brigadier, and I don't think they're that far away. They're hiding from everybody, not just from us. From the rest of the gang, from the other shepherds on the mountain, from everybody. They're frightened for their lives and they're hiding without intelligence, without plans, in any hole they can find, like animals. But they must have found some shelter because you can't survive up here without it, and only you know this mountain well enough to tell me where they've found it. Now tell me!'

'I don't know . . . There's La Selletta, that's the next village—or it used to be, but it's a good walk from here, best part of two hours, and it's completely bombed out except for the church.'

'The church still has a roof on it?'

'Not the church hasn't, but the sacristy . . . and then there's a sort of crypt. A family held out there for four weeks at the end of the war with only a tub full of water and some—'

The Captain had switched on his radio and was already talking to one of the helicopter pilots, telling him they should land down in the valley and then be ready to pick everyone up at La Selletta in approximately two hours. They would go on foot. You couldn't surprise a mountain but you could surprise two frightened fugitives.

The dog-handlers gathered.

'You don't want us to go on looking for the girl's body?'

'I need you with me.'

The walk was long and arduous. They had to fight against the wind which took their breath away. No one spoke except the Brigadier, who felt he should keep Bacci going by breathlessly recounting wartime stories to him since he looked so exhausted and depressed.

'A tub full of water and a bag of wrinkled vegetables. It was supposed to be a miracle—at one time people used to come up here—but my father who lived up here until the bombing said they'd a ham hidden away—that they hadn't told anybody about . . . Keep straight on towards the ridge—I'll be with you in a minute.'

And he would fall back to check on the boy who had been sick.

After about an hour the high wind dropped, only returning in occasional gusts that sprayed them with raindrops. When they neared the ridge they saw that it rose on the opposite side of a valley. Below them lay the remains of the church, the roof of the nave missing. What had once been a paved square in front of it now looked like an overgrown lawn. The Captain was speaking into his radio.

'This cloud's coming down.'

It was rolling away from them down the side of the mountain.

'We can see it.'

'You'll still be able to pick us up?'

'We'll do our best. How much longer will you be?'

He looked at the Brigadier for an answer.

'We're here.'

'A few minutes,' the Captain said, and switched off.

A small cluster of buildings clung on to the wall of the church, behind the exposed altar stones that had scraps of bright blue mosaic stuck here and there. A trickle of woodsmoke was winding its way crookedly upwards.

The men were deployed in silence, the handlers and dogs grouped out of the way. Bacci was sent to the very edge of the near side of the valley where he crouched behind a huge flint boulder and tried to keep his feet steady on the eroded ground. To his left the mountainside dropped almost vertically until it reached another valley a hundred metres or so lower down. The rusty corrugated roof of some sort of shed jutted out half way down the drop. In the bottom were the roofless ruins of the houses. The inhabitants of La Selletta had built their church on the highest patch of flat ground.

Bacci caught a glimpse of the green-clad men slipping silently round the other side of the church. It was quite difficult to distinguish them in the green-grey gloom of the late afternoon. Then he looked at the jumble of buildings at the rear of the church and saw a light that flickered and then vanished. There was a window in one of the jutting walls, a small barred window. Concentrating his gaze there, he managed to make out that the flickering light came from a fire, and that it disappeared when somebody passed in front of it. There were two people in the room, though he could only see their heads and the top half of their bodies. One figure stood motionless, wrapped in something dark. The other was moving agitatedly about the room, sometimes blocking the dull red light of the fire. Then they came together and the dark covering dropped from the still figure.

After the first shock of seeing the girl's white flesh, Bacci tried to tear his eyes away, to contact the Captain, to stop the attack somehow. But he had no radio and he didn't dare move. Wisps of damp cloud were moving slowly around him, clinging to him and making everything look unreal in the thick silence. There was no longer anybody in sight except for the figures moving in the square of flickering light, and they might have been a hundred kilometres away, they were so cut off from him. He saw them lie down, clinging to each other more like frightened children than like lovers. His nerves were stretched painfully with the strain of wanting to stop everything until it was over, but out of the corner of his eyes he caught a swift movement. The men in green were creeping out of the mist and becoming visible in a circle around the roofless church.

'No . . .' whispered Bacci, his mouth close to the flint boulder. 'No . . .'

The Captain must have known, or at least suspected, about the girl . . . But he couldn't know what was happening in there. Nobody else knew. Nobody else could see because there was only the one window. The circle was edging closer, diminishing. There was no sound at all. The two figures were moving desperately as if they knew how little time was left to them. One of the men in green raised his arm.

'No . . .!' whispered Bacci, and he tried to make a signal. He lost his footing on the slope and grabbed the boulder, kicking out. A big piece of flint dislodged itself and hurtled down to hit the rusty metal roof below with a whang that echoed across the whole mountain before it bounced away into the cloud.

Rudolfo, half-dressed and armed with a rifle, shot out through the open nave and leaped across some fallen beams.

'Hold your fire!' The order came out of the mist. Rudolfo crashed through the circle of men and vanished in the grey cloud.

'Loose the dogs!'

They had him handcuffed within four minutes.

Bacci was still behind the boulder, his eyes fixed on the crouching white figure in the firelit room. He saw the men go in and saw that she didn't move but let them cover her and pick her up.

He didn't see her again because she was surrounded by other people after that, but over the noise of the radios and the helicopters that were circling, trying to find them, he heard her screaming and screaming at them to let Rudolfo go.

CHAPTER 12

The Captain was reading quietly in his office. It was Easter Sunday morning, and apart from the two men in the communications room who were chatting with the cars on patrol the building was almost empty.

After a freak hailstorm two days ago the weather had finally settled down and the sun shone out of a tranquil blue sky. The Captain unbuttoned his jacket and finished reading the autopsy report. Caldini, the gamekeeper, had died from the stab wounds but the damage to his eyes had been done before that. He set the report aside and picked up Rudolfo's statement.

Answered to Questions:
I don't know Pratesi, Giuseppe. I know that he has a sausage factory near Pontino but I've never seen him. As far as I know he has nothing to do with this kidnapping.

A.Q.: In January of this year, I don't know the exact date, Caldini, Mario, gamekeeper at the villa, came to see me on the mountain to tell me that the villa was being sold. I know Caldini because I graze the paddocks at the villa in summer and use the stables there, and because he hunts on the mountain on Sundays and comes into my house to eat. When I need money he buys a lamb from me. Caldini told me that the new owner of the villa intended to evict us both and that he was going to build a swimming pool in the field that I use to grow food, and that there was nothing I could do because I have no contract. The next Sunday Caldini brought a man called Garau, Pasqualino, with him. He said Garau knew the daughter of the man who was buying the villa and that they were Americans. He said GARAU knew how to organize a kidnapping but that the risk was too big because he was known to the police. CALDINI said we could save my summer grazing and his house by a mock kidnapping. GARAU told me that the girl could easily be hidden in my house because it's on the mountain and because I have no police record, and that we couldn't be prosecuted if we didn't ask for a ransom. We planned to frighten this man into not buying the villa.

A.Q.: I don't know of any other person who wanted to buy the villa.

A.Q.: As far as I know there was no ransom asked for.

A.Q.: I went down the mountain on the day it snowed. SCANO, Bastianino, drove me to Florence in a truck. I don't know who the truck belonged to. We went by the back road. The back road is the old road from Pontino that passes by the villa. Nobody saw us. SCANO left me in Piazza Pitti and went back to wait for me at the stable I use at the villa. I got into the courtyard and hid myself in the car. It wasn't locked. GARAU had watched the girl for almost a month. He told me what to do.

A.Q.: SCANO, Bastianino, was dressed normally when I left him.

A.Q.: I don't know who brought the food up the mountain. I picked it up from the same place twice a week. There was always another guard with me at the house, sometimes GARAU and sometimes SCANO, Bastianino. The gamekeeper came up twice to hunt.

The Captain broke off and looked towards the window. Once he realized what a fool the gang had made of him Rudolfo had refused to speak. The second interrogation had been a waste of time, and the next day they had been forced to give up and take his statement.

> A.Q.: I left my house and took the girl to La Selleta on Palm Sunday. I don't know what the date was. There was nobody else in the house when we left. Later the Carabinieri arrested me at La Selletta.

That was all. He wouldn't even speak to the barrister they had given him. His hands had been trembling when they put the handcuffs back on him to take him away. Once he had cried, beating his head on his knees. Once, when they had tried to pressurize him into talking for his own good, he had screamed for his mother.

He was nineteen years old, the same age as the boy who had been sick behind the bushes at the sight of a dead man with his eyes pushed out; the same age as Deborah Maxwell.

The Captain had tried to talk to Maxwell, to explain to him about the Stockholm Syndrome, to help him understand that the link between captor and captive took time and patience to break, and that a statement full of lies and contradictions designed to protect the kidnappers was not unusual. After two hours he had given up, having at least dissuaded him from bringing a charge of rape which could only have been more damaging to his daughter than to Rudolfo.

Mrs Maxwell had come back to see him.

'I want to understand, to help her if I can.'

'I'm sure you can. Be patient.'

'But you can't mean that Debbie was in love with that bandit. I saw him. Why, he wasn't even clean. Debbie . . . What you said about her being frightened of the others and that he was kinder to her. I can understand that. And if he fed her all the time and she was dependent on him, I can understand her trying to defend him, but not . . . You don't know Debbie.'

'I know about kidnappings.' He had told them about the cocaine but not about anything else. It was over now, anyway. 'Try not to make her feel guilty afterwards, when she becomes normal.'

'How long . . .?'

'Perhaps a month. I shall have to take another statement from her when she feels ready to talk to me.'

'She looked so wild. Her hair all tangled, and her eyes . . . I'll never forget her eyes and the smell of her when I—that wasn't Debbie.'

'Please don't worry. It's over.'

He had telephoned her the next day.

'How is she?'

'I'm sure she's a little better—but sometimes she watches us. I can feel her watching us. I don't know if you understand what I mean.'

'I understand.'

'In her sleep she talks in Italian. We sat by her all night, John and I. And today she said to me, "I'm hungry," just like that, and it wasn't mealtime. Maybe she's getting better. She wouldn't eat before.'

'Don't expect too much.' How many times over the years had he repeated these stock phrases? Not that it mattered much what he said, so long as he was calm.

'I've thought over everything you said. I'm probably being foolish but I can't help thinking of all the songs, love songs, you know what I mean, that talk about chains and being captured. I don't know why it came into my head but it did. And feeding always forms part of courtship—I read an article . . . You probably think I'm being very foolish . . .'

'No, no . . .'

'I'm trying to understand how Debbie could have—'

'Just stay close to her.'

He looked down again now at the mountain of papers that had to be read and signed. With an effort he might finish this morning. He picked up the stack of typed transcripts from the readable parts of the girl's exercise book. The typing was hurried and the translation was imperfect, but it would serve for now. Another transcript would be made when the lab had finished washing the pages. The first sheet contained part of a letter to Katrine Nilsen.

1 . . . speak to each other the whole time it was happening, do you realize that? Nobody will tell me where they've taken you. Nobody speaks English and I don't understand their Italian. For three days I didn't speak at all. I was waiting for them to kill me, just lying still and waiting. There are so many things I want to write to you even if it's only in this exercise book. They haven't taken any of my things, not even my watch, but I can only write when there's enough light from the fire. I want to . . .
OMISSIS. Ten lines obliterated/Cont . . .

2 . . . have imagined that I could have lived through anything as frightening as this but I go on sleeping and waking and even eating. What difference could it have made to them to leave us together? All day I've been thinking about what it will be like when we're free. I want us to go on a trip together. I want us to laugh the way we laughed at that restaurant on Jacqueline's birthday because she couldn't remember the end of the joke she tried to tell us and got it wrong in three languages. Laughing like that without thinking or caring about anything. Now I can't even imagine how anyone can laugh that way. I never knew the world could be as sad and ugly as this. If I'd known I would never have been unhappy, even for an hour. Now there isn't any light and the people I see have no faces. I don't want to die here where nobody knows me. Nobody comes near me except with food and . . .
OMISSIS. Eight lines obliterated.

3. *9th March*
I haven't eaten anything for two days. I'm not afraid of dying any more but I refuse to be slaughtered like an animal in this dark hole. They don't speak to me except for the young one. I hate them all. There's even a child here sometimes, with his face covered.
10th March
God help me. *Somebody* help me. I don't want to die. If this is a punishment for all the things I've done then I only have to bear it and wait. I think this is the saddest place in the world. All morning the wind was moaning and now I can hear rain. I can hear it coming in through the roof and everything feels damp and cold. I cried for so long today that now I feel totally empty. I don't ask myself any more why I'm crying. Sometimes it's only because I want to hear my own voice. Last night I cried only a little because of the cramps I had and because I didn't know how to ask for what I needed but they knew anyway and had everything. I was so cold and shivery that he gave me a sheepskin. I keep it over my legs away from my face because of the smell.
11th March
I asked them for some clean clothes. I asked *him*. I hate all of them. I never knew I could feel so much anger. I hate them not just for this but for every bad thing that ever happened to me. I'm only frightened of one of them. The fat one who . . .
OMISSIS. Two lines cancelled.
. . . *he* said I mustn't be afraid, that they won't hurt me and that you'll come and take me home. I don't understand the other things he says. Please come soon because I don't think I can . . .
OMISSIS. Two pages obliterated.

4. Page contains an Italian/English vocabulary. Some of the words have sketches next to them. Last six lines obliterated.

5 . . . made me listen to the radio. I heard my name but I couldn't understand anything else because it was too fast. They blindfolded me because somebody came. I know who it was. It was the fat one. I will never forget his voice. Please God whatever else happens to me don't let them leave me alone with him. If it happens I know what to do, if I only have the courage. I think about it every day so that if the moment comes I won't be frightened. Today *he* gave me a newborn lamb to hold. It's the first living thing I've touched since I've been here. How could such a trivial thing make me so happy? It kept thrusting its muzzle at my neck to look for milk. I pulled the sheepskin right up to our noses to keep us warm. It rained all day again. *He* has just put some wood on the fire. It sizzles and the room is full of smoke. They . . .
OMISSIS. Eight lines obliterated/Cont . . .

6 . . . eat everything they give me because I want to live. I want to get out of this place into the light but there's no sign from you. What if nobody ever finds out where I am? At night I try to remember some of the prayers we said at school but all I can think of saying is God help me, God help me, over and over.

19th March
Even if it is a punishment it's *too much*. I can't have deserved anything as bad as this. I suffer so much from the dark that I think if they would let me out for one day I would come back. Just one day so that I start hoping again. If you leave me here too long I won't be able to survive because people can only stand just so much loneliness and despair.

20th March
Every morning and evening he brings the lamb in to warm it and feed it from a bottle like a baby. It can't walk because it is lame on its back legs.
OMISSIS. Eight lines obliterated.

7 . . . just one word because I can't stand any more. The fat one came. They didn't blindfold me because he had put on a black skiing mask like the others. I could see his eyes. I know now that I can do it. There's so much anger inside me like a big burning black thing. He killed the lamb, the fat one, right outside the door so that I would hear it die. Afterwards they made me eat some of it. I want so much to tell the truth about everything.
OMISSIS [the words "I wanted to eat the lamb. I lied to Katrine about Christmas" have been partially cancelled.] If I ever get out I'll tell the truth. He gave me the radio to listen to but there was nothing on the news that I could understand.

22nd March
Every morning I watch him bring in the milk and drop the yellow stuff from the dusty bottle into it. Then he beats it with a spiky stick. The movements are always exactly the same. I have learned a lot of words in Italian that I don't know in English. They are not in my school dictionary. Asked him why but he doesn't know. Maybe because it's too small. Every evening I hear the sheep coming with their bells at exactly the same time. Then he brings in the milk exactly forty-five minutes later. If only the others would go away I would wait here quietly and do exactly what he said even when he wasn't there. I wouldn't try to escape. I would do as I was told and be patient until it was all over and . . .
OMISSIS. Seven lines obliterated.
[The margin of this page has a childish drawing of a house with a pointed roof and smoke coming out of the chimney. Two figures inside the house. A chain and padlock round the outer edge.]

8. Drawing of the sun with long rays in left-hand margin. The last page of the exercise book contains another Italian /English vocabulary.

Two pages have been torn from the centre of the book.

The Captain stapled the pages together and put them to one side. The diary stopped before the date of Maxwell's message with the three questions. It had been to her stepmother that she had run that evening here in his office. Nevertheless, the journalists had photographed the three of them together in their suite at the Excelsior the next morning.

He had questioned the girl in the afternoon but her father had been there to interrupt her if he thought she was going to say anything dangerous. She was still deeply shocked and he had asked her only simple, direct questions.

Did Rudolfo save your life? Do you understand that if you refuse to say so he'll be accused of murder?

Did the fat man attack you?

Did you know how to defend yourself?

Do you remember who gave you the wild flowers?

Did you see Rudolfo come up behind him with a knife?

She had looked at her father, terrified not of the Captain but of saying the wrong thing. The second time there had been an English-speaking lawyer there, too.

Did Rudolfo start unchaining you as soon as the second guard stopped coming?

She couldn't have managed the walk to La Selletta after being immobile for almost a month.

He had dug out the article that had appeared in a police magazine two years ago. There was a photograph of the New York sergeant with a quote underneath. "It's the simplest, most effective defence there is; you just dig your thumbs in to the eye sockets. But most women wouldn't do it."

Not to defend herself from rape perhaps, but if her life were at stake?

According to Garau's statement they had talked of killing her if the risk became too great. He had nothing to lose in saying so since he had been in prison when the gamekeeper was killed.

And Scano's boy had been picked up that same afternoon in a bar down in the city:

I intend to answer. I intend to tell the truth.

A.Q.: We were in difficulty because of the death of PILADU who had taken an overdose. It was the gamekeeper who decided it was safest to get rid of the girl once we had fixed for the ransom to be paid. She was still there when I left on Sunday morning, and he came up to relieve me. We were short of guards since GARAU had been arrested after a fight.

A.Q.: I don't know what the fight with the scarred man was about. It's possible that he suspected something and wanted a share because he had introduced the girl to GARAU but I don't know.

A.Q.: I know PRATESI, Giuseppe, because he has a factory near Pontino. Everybody knows him. I don't know whether GARAU re-cycled money for him though I know he did re-cycle money because he told me so, sometimes through drugs, sometimes through an arms dealer. I think the dealer was Sicilian but I don't know. I don't know the names of any of the people GARAU dealt with. I know he took a percentage of the money but I don't know how much. GARAU was to re-cycle the ransom money.

A.Q.: The cloak I wore in Piazza Pitti was Rudolfo's. I asked him to lend it to me because it was snowing. I told him I was cold. The pipes are my father's, I can't play them. I had them hidden in the back of the truck. I don't remember who the truck belonged to. GARAU borrowed it. We planned to make Rudolfo take the blame if anything went wrong, he's a bit simple.

A.Q.: I have only ever bought heroin for my own use.

The telephone rang.

'Marshal Guarnaccia at Pitti, sir.'

'Put him through. Good morning, Marshal. I thought you might have gone home to Syracuse.'

'No, no. It's not much over six weeks since I was last home. My mother died . . . And since my Brigadier's just got married I thought he should have Easter . . . I rang you because I remembered something that might tie up a loose end for you, something I saw.'

'Yes?'

'Garau—Baffetti, as they call him—was caught stealing clothes from the Prisoners' Assistance at the Appeal Courts. I was there for something else but I caught sight of him slipping out through the gate and the woman there said it was the day for women's clothing not men's.'

'I see. That's why the Maxwells couldn't identify all the clothing we found in Rudolfo's house. We knew they hadn't come from Demontis's sister-in-law who's short and fat.'

'Did you find Demontis?'

'Easily. Needless to say the sister-in-law wouldn't shelter him and we found him in Scano's hen house.'

'What about the girl? Has she said anything?'

'Practically nothing. Her father won't let her.'

'It's been a messy case.'

'Very. How's Cipolla?'

'He's better, but he'll try again. For somebody like Baffetti who's as at home in prison as out it's one thing, but fifteen years inside for Cipolla . . . He'll try again. He's nothing to hope for. He hasn't even any children. A man should have children. You must be snowed under with paperwork.'

'I have been but I hope to finish this morning.'

'I'm going to go out for a breath of air while things are quiet.'

'You won't be able to get through the streets!'

'I shan't go towards the centre. I shall take a stroll down the river.'

'If you cross over you might call in here. I'd like a word with you about Rudolfo.'

'Have you talked to the Brigadier?'

'I have, but now he's away on holiday. Their new Marshal's arrived.'

'Well . . . I might look in.'

'If you should be over this side of the river.'

The Captain worked on for another half-hour before stopping to stretch his legs and make a decision. He would never get anywhere trying to make Maxwell see his point of view. He had no choice but to insist on seeing the girl alone. She needed to talk to someone anyway for her own good. He sat down again and picked up the telephone.

'Get me Mr Maxwell at the Excelsior.'

When he got through a voice said:

'I'm sorry, sir, Mr Maxwell and his family checked out yesterday evening.'

'Checked out? Do you know where they've gone?'

'I think they've gone back to America.'

'Thank you.'

He put the receiver down and sat for a moment looking at his fingers on the edge of the desk. The headache, which he only now noticed had subsided, was coming back again. Even if he had known he could hardly have stopped them. The evidence was all against Rudolfo, and the girl had suffered enough already. It would have taken at least a month to get at the truth, and he had no licence to kidnap the victims of kidnappings. The Nilsen girl had only stayed because the kidnappers had instructed her to stay.

He felt defeated, partly by the squalid bunch he had

arrested who, after all, had succeeded in making Rudolfo take most of the blame, and partly by Maxwell, because the Maxwells of this world were a law unto themselves. At least, he reflected wryly, it was a change from feeling defeated by the magistracy.

He fished a series of telephone numbers out of his top pocket and tried a few of them, discounting the ones he knew were restaurants since it was too early.

The fourth try was successful.

'I thought you'd want to know, Maxwell's left.'

'For America?'

'Yes.'

'Then you'll have to follow him.'

'Yes. Preferably in about three weeks' time. I think she'll want to talk to me. I have strong hopes that first she'll talk to her stepmother who'll get in touch with me. In the meantime, I'll be finished with the paperwork today and will send the files to you tomorrow. The case can go under Instruction.'

'I'll ring the Instructing Judge in the morning.'

Fusarri put the receiver down and dropped his head back on the pillow. The sun was shining through the outer shutters, making stripes across the tangled white sheets.

'Who was it?' asked a drowsy voice beside him.

'Carabinieri.'

'Do you have to go out?'

'No, no. They don't need me any more . . . if they ever did.' He gazed up at the cherubs disporting themselves on the frescoed ceiling. 'Some of those fellows frighten me to death.'

'Rubbish . . . I don't believe you.'

'You haven't seen Maestrangelo. I think he's the most serious man I've ever met.'

'So are you serious.' She roused herself sufficiently to drop a kiss on his shoulder.

'Only when I'm with you.'

'Ooh, now you're being ridiculous!'

'I'm not being ridiculous at all,' he said gravely. 'Come here . . . that's better. This is what life is for.'

There was no hint of irony in his voice, and not the least suggestion in his look that he might just as easily have been somewhere else.

The Marshal passed only a few tourists who were checking street names against their guidebooks and making for the centre and the Cathedral. For the rest, there was nobody much about except one or two people from his Quarter, women hurrying back from nine-thirty Mass to get the mixed roast on for Easter dinner, and small groups of men in Sunday suits but without ties gossiping outside the Communist club. The bars were hung with forests of foil-wrapped eggs and there were tiny pink and yellow sugar eggs stacked in the windows.

''Morning, Marshal.'

''Morning.'

'Happy Easter.'

At the corner of Piazza Santo Spirito an old man with a flower in his buttonhole was selling daffodils and lilies from big plastic buckets on a stone ledge.

Some of the very tiny streets were quite empty.

He crossed the river at Ponte alla Carraia and paused a moment to watch the canoes and skiffs passing underneath in the olive-green water. A dozen or so men were fishing by the weir.

He hadn't intended to walk as far as Il Prato but an echoing drumroll in the distance and a glimpse of silk flags spinning up between the buildings into the light attracted him. He got there too late. Families were dispersing and the giant three-tiered doors were being closed. Two men in orange jackets were clearing up the mess left in the road by the white bulls. One of the animals had lost a big blue plastic flower from its garland.

The Marshal would quite like to have seen the pagoda-shaped cart set off for the Cathedral since it was the first time he had stayed for Easter, but by now it might well have reached the streets near the centre where thousands of people were waiting for it, and with the fire-engine going along behind he had little chance of seeing anything but the top of it. In any case, he'd better call in at Headquarters seeing as he was on that side of the river. Once he had sent a postcard of it to the boys. One of the town hall workers, dressed up as peasants in leather jerkins and straw hats, was holding on to a bull by its gilded horn. The boys had been disappointed because they'd wanted a picture of the cart exploding. Perhaps he would find one later today when things quietened down.

He ought to speak his mind to the Captain about young Bacci but he probably wouldn't. The Captain worked the boy too hard. There was no harm in him making a career for himself but that wasn't everything. He ought to find a nice Italian girl and settle down, stop him making a fool of himself. But if he was working seven days a week what could you expect?

The Marshal ambled slowly on. Perhaps he would say something after all.

For Rudolfo he knew there was nothing to be done. Another shepherd was taking care of his sheep and the younger brother had gone back to Sardinia.

Rudolfo was lying in an overcrowded cell, staring up across the room at a small barred square with an even smaller square of blue in its top left-hand corner. When the other four had invited him to join their card game he hadn't answered, or else he hadn't heard. One of the players, a Neapolitan, had laughed and said, 'Let him be, if he won't speak. Sardinians are all alike. Another card . . .'

Rudolfo turned on his blanket and stared at the pitted wall.

OTHER TITLES IN THE SOHO CRIME SERIES

JANWILLEM VAN DE WETERING

Outsider in Amsterdam
Tumbleweed
The Corpse on the Dike
The Japanese Corpse
The Blond Baboon
The Maine Massacre
Just a Corpse at Twilight
The Streetbird
The Hollow-Eyed Angel
The Mind-Murders
Hard Rain
The Perfidious Parrot
The Amsterdam Cops: Collected Stories

SEICHŌ MATSUMOTO
Inspector Imanishi Investigates

PATRICIA CARLON
The Souvenir
The Running Woman
Crime of Silence
The Price of an Orphan
The Unquiet Night
Hush, It's a Game
Death by Demonstration
Who Are You, Linda Condrick?

PETER LOVESEY
The Vault
The Last Detective
On the Edge
The Reaper
Rough Cider
The False Inspector Dew
Diamond Dust
Diamond Solitaire
The House Sitter
The Summons
Bloodhounds
Upon a Dark Night
The Circle

MAGDALEN NABB
Property of Blood
Death of an Englishman
Some Bitter Taste
The Marshal and the Madwoman
The Marshal and the Murderer
Death in Autumn

CHERYL BENARD
Moghul Buffet

QIU XIAOLONG
Death of a Red Heroine
A Loyal Character Dancer
When Red is Black

J. ROBERT JANES
Sandman
Mayhem
Mannequin
Carousel
Kaleidoscope
Dollmaker

AKIMITSU TAKAGI
The Informer
The Tattoo Murder Case

STAN JONES
White Sky, Black Ice
Shaman Pass

TIMOTHY WATTS
Cons
Money Lovers

HELEN TURSTEN
Detective Inspector Huss

MARTIN LIMÓN
Jade Lady Burning
Slicky Boys
Buddha's Money

CARA BLACK
Murder in the Marais
Murder in Belleville
Murder in the Sentier
Murder in the Bastille
Murder in Clichy

TOD GOLDBERG
Living Dead Girl

REBECCA PAWEL
Death of a Nationalist
Law of Return

CLAIRE FRANCIS
A Dark Devotion